DRIED FRESH FLOWERS

When to Pick and How to Dry

DRIED FRESH FLOWERS

When to Pick and How to Dry

ELIZABETH BULLIVANT

PELHAM BOOKS

Acknowledgements

For me, writing a book has been a totally new experience and somewhat of a surprise for my family, without whose active help and criticism there would not have been any legible order to my midnight scribblings.

A very big 'thank you' to my son, George and daughter-in-law Sarah for their many hours of typing, re-typing and rearranging, until the book took shape.

Phil Bishop not only spent hours and many films taking photographs for me to choose from but so willingly gave me advice and help without which I would never have succeeded with my own camera.

Many thanks, too, to Doreen Hill for her delightful seedhead drawings and to Nadia Brydon for her excellent detailed and instructive ones.

Photographers Eric Crichton, Jacqui Hurst, Lorna Rose and Susan Witney have generously provided most useful additions to the book.

Last but not least my grateful thanks go to my energetic, enthusiastic and encouraging husband, Anthony, who cheerfully suffers late meals and dried flowers everywhere.

PELHAM BOOKS

Published by the Penguin Group
27 Wrights Lane, London W8 5TZ, England
Viking Penguin Inc., 40 West 23rd Street, New York, New York 10010, USA
Penguin Books Australia Ltd, Ringwood, Victoria, Australia
Penguin Books Canada Ltd, 2801 John Street, Markham, Ontario, Canada L3R 1B4
Penguin Books (NZ) Ltd, 182–190 Wairau Road, Auckland 10, New Zealand

Penguin Books Ltd, Registered Offices: Harmondsworth, Middlesex, England

First published 1989
Reprinted 1991

Typeset in 10/12pt Garamond ITC by Goodfellow & Egan, Cambridge
Colour reproduction by Anglia Graphics, Bedford
Printed and bound in Italy by L.E.G.O.

ISBN 0 7207 1854 6

A CIP catalogue record for this book is available from the British Library
LIBRARY OF CONGRESS CATALOG NUMBER
89–60531

CONTENTS

INTRODUCTION

THE GARDEN OUTSIDE has been deep and white with snow for over a week, with the lowest temperatures for decades. The electricity is off and the greenhouse frozen, and yet our rooms are bright and fresh with summer flowers and will continue to be so during the months to come. Yes – dried fresh flowers from our own garden! In the winter months they are a glorious reminder of summer, and in the summer the knowledgeable gardener will marvel that you have all your summer flowers out at the same time.

I am asked, 'How do you do it?' 'Do you dry them with chemicals?' 'Do you tint them and dye them?' Goodness gracious me, no! Nothing difficult, nothing complicated!

Light from the snow reflecting on to an arrangement of
mixed perennials, annuals, glycerined and dried foliage,
seed heads and grasses in a colourful winter arrangement.

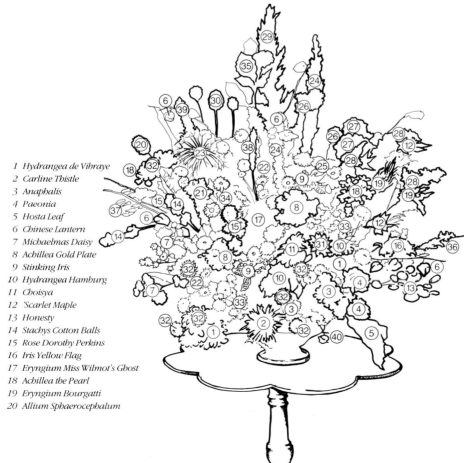

1 Hydrangea de Vibraye
2 Carline Thistle
3 Anaphalis
4 Paeonia
5 Hosta Leaf
6 Chinese Lantern
7 Michaelmas Daisy
8 Achillea Gold Plate
9 Stinking Iris
10 Hydrangea Hamburg
11 Choisya
12 'Scarlet Maple
13 Honesty
14 Stachys Cotton Balls
15 Rose Dorothy Perkins
16 Iris Yellow Flag
17 Eryngium Miss Wilmot's Ghost
18 Achillea the Pearl
19 Eryngium Bourgatti
20 Allium Sphaerocephalum

21 Primula Florindae
22 Greater Knapweed
23 Allium Albopilosum
24 Delphinium
25 Hydrangea Veitchii
26 Centaurea Macrocephala
27 Leek
28 Golden Rod
29 Pampas Grass
30 Echinops – Blue Balls
31 Artichoke
32 Helichrysum
33 Ammohium
34 Acroclinium
35 Glycerined Beech
36 Old Man's Beard
37 Radish Seed Heads
38 Wheat
39 Aruncus
40 Shoo Fly

There is nothing difficult about drying many garden flowers, including hydrangeas; but that was not in my mind thirty years ago on a sunny September day, as my husband and I sat on the edge of the black and yellow tiled terrace in front of this house and gazed in amazement at the huge clump of forget-me-not-blue hydrangeas, with their massive heads firmly in command above the nettles and brambles.

We were wondering if we liked this house, which was for sale, and if we could cope with the overgrown garden and shrubbery, all smothered with ground elder, nettles and brambles, and how on earth we would ever get the deep mossy hayfield back to being a lawn again. I only had to look at the blue hydrangeas (and this was a very unusual light blue) to know what the answer was – yes. Blue is my favourite colour. I had never met up with hydrangeas in a garden before. All my life I had been used to a chalky garden, where of course they would not grow.

At that time I did not realize what a task it would be, albeit a very enjoyable one, to reclaim the garden. During our years with the Army I had longed for and dreamed of having a garden that smelt delicious, tasted delicious and looked delightful. I was fed up with planting plants and sowing seeds only to be moved to another house, and often to another continent, before they had time to flower or be eaten. There was a limit to the number of pots of lilies or plants we could cram into the car, with baggage and children as well, and it was always tiresome to have to get a permit from the ministry when we brought them back to Britain. So the thought of a garden where the lilies could grow undisturbed and where blue hydrangeas would grow as well was my idea of heaven.

In those days I knew nothing about drying flowers. I had a romantic vision of a garden of Eden full of daffodils, tulips, scented hyacinths and violets, honeysuckle, wisteria, lilac, syringa, sweet peas and roses (and now I could add hydrangeas), all flowering together all year round in permanent sunshine!

Once we owned the house and garden, the reality of rain, wind, frost and weeds stirred childhood memories. I had pre-war memories of a large four-acre walled garden, with two wide herbaceous borders down the centre dividing the prolific vegetable plots and leading to the south-facing high wall, clothed in delicious white-fleshed peaches, from which we children were allowed to eat as many windfalls as we liked. When I was a child, the garden was looked after by an expert head gardener and his team of under-gardeners. Gradually I began to remember seeing them growing and tending the different types of flowers and vegetables, and I was now able to try out these ideas for myself and discover it was not quite as simple as it had looked.

I thought back with renewed guilt and a great deal of sympathy to a spring Sunday morning when my mother, who was a great gardener, invited her friends to come back with her after church and look at her large and lovingly tended rockery, which was a patchwork of scented colour. At the time I was seven years old and had a very strong three-quarter-grown lamb called Jane, which I had reared on a bottle. Normally she was tethered on a rough piece of lawn and had a large Swiss cow-bell attached to her collar.

As we approached the part of the garden where the rockery was, I gradually became aware of the fact that the Swiss cow-bell seemed to be there too! I followed fearfully as my mother led her friends triumphantly round the last corner and into view of her floral masterpiece. It had gone! In its place was a huge, bloated, woolly sheep, standing bleating on the topmost rock. Then, loudly clanging the cow-bell, she bounced down over the rockery stones and came to greet me. My mother was speechless with horror. Her friends, however, although very sympathetic, thought it

A large bank of the sky-blue hydrangea 'Générale Vicomtesse de Vibraye', the flowers of which will all be dried in the autumn.

very funny, so Jane and I did not get into quite as much trouble as we might have done.

Soon after this episode, when I was eight, my real gardening education started, although I was not aware of this at the time.

In those days there was no school near by, so I was taught the three Rs by a governess. When my brother went to boarding school, a new governess took on the thankless task of trying to interest me in things other than my pony and pets, climbing trees, and making houses under the syringa bushes, where there were secret paths through the stinging nettles to aid the smuggling of quantities of apples out of the kitchen garden past the gardeners, hidden in the voluminous elasticated legs of my navy-blue knickers.

Gravy, as I called the new governess, turned out to be a keen member of the British Wildflower Society. Starting on 1 March, we set out to scour the countryside for as many wild flowers actually in bloom as we could find. Then with the help of *The British Flora* by Bentham and Hooker, a wonderful work that has detailed drawings of wild flowers in one volume and botanical descriptions in the second, we entered the name of each flower, together with the date and where we found it, into a book specially provided by the Society.

During the next two summers lessons were interspersed with exciting trips, sometimes including a picnic, to different environments; Portland Bill, for example, which is like an enormous rockery, and Bovington Heath, where we found acid-loving plants such as heathers and sundews and the extraordinary rambling pink dodder. On the chalk downs we found and identified totally different flowers, such as wild rock roses, saxifrages and the beautiful blue milkwort and squinanciwort, but the most thrilling of all were the bee orchid and other orchids. In lakes and ponds and beside rivers we found another world of flowers, including the elegant pink flowering rush, bulrushes, yellow water lilies and irises and highly scented mints.

Gravy showed me how to identify exactly which variety we had found by examining the leaves, the parts of the flower and the seed pods. It was all like a wonderful treasure hunt.

Now, many years later, as we continue to create our garden here, I find it is of immense help when I acquire a new plant to think back to those childhood days and remember where I found something similar growing in its natural habitat. I can then choose a suitable place for it here in the garden.

During the first year here we began to resurrect the old rectory garden. I spent every available moment outside, discovering the joy and satisfaction of clearing the soil of ground elder and bindweed, discovering interesting plants already growing, and experimenting with new ones grown from cuttings or from seed.

With the help of our gardener, Tom, and his wife Dorothy, we turned the hayfield back into a lawn. We rescued the blue hydrangeas and also many pink ones from the brambles, and were thrilled to find lots of hidden rhododendrons and azaleas. Tom had worked in the rectory garden for over thirty years until about eighteen months before we bought it from the Church. His wife had worked in the house part-time, but much preferred to help her husband in the garden.

In the autumn, to my surprise, one or two strangers came to the door to ask for hydrangeas to dry. It appeared that in the past they had been given them to mix with other flowers that they had dried. So it was the blue hydrangeas that started our dried flower business, and there is nothing difficult and nothing complicated about drying them. You just pick them at the right time, strip off the leaves, and hang them up near your hot water boiler!

As the years went by, as well as discovering what plants already grew in the garden, we were given new varieties and we grew a lot from cuttings and many more from seed. Gradually we found that many ordinary garden flowers would dry at some stage of their growth, and we were able to make attractive dried arrangements from them. One day a friend came for some dried fresh flowers. She was accompanied by her sister, who worked in a large store in London's West End, and suggested that I gave her some samples to show to the manageress of the garden department. This was very exciting, but what on earth could I use to send a collection of dried fresh flowers to the West End? Luckily I managed to find a Women's Institute cake bag and an empty cellophane-fronted shirt bag left from my husband's last birthday. Into these I packed a collection of all sorts of dried flowers, seed heads and grasses, including of course the blue hydrangeas.

To my surprise there was an order for twelve bunches by return of post! We were in business! Now our flowers go far and wide, both in England and overseas.

1
DRIED FRESH FLOWERS

I F THIS WAS A cookery recipe for a dried flower arrangement it might begin with 'First grow your flowers for drying.' But it is not necessary to start like that, because if you possess a garden, no matter how small, you are sure to already have a lot of flowers that will dry.

There is nothing more attractive than a fresh bowl of flowers and foliage picked from one's own herbaceous borders and shrubs. How lovely they are for a few days while fresh, and how sad

Fresh or dried? A vase of dried fresh flowers that look as if
they have just been picked from the garden.

A part of the garden where most of the plants will provide excellent material for
drying. Purple honesty, yellow iris and aquilegia are grown for their seed pods,
while the hostas provide both seed pods and leaves. The red plumes of the astilbe
will also be dried. In the background is a tall yellow broom for drying in flower,
and pink lupins will give early seed heads in July.

and what a waste it is when they have to be thrown out at the end of the week because they have
died. Well, a lot of these flowers could have been saved if they had been picked at the right time
and dried, and your arrangement would have lasted for many months and probably years.

In these days of very hot, centrally heated houses, fresh cut flowers last just a few days and
can be a very costly item in a weekly budget. Dried flowers, on the other hand, positively love a hot
dry atmosphere, and come to no harm if you go on holiday for several weeks and cannot attend to
them. They will still be as good when you return.

What an ideal present they are to give to your favourite bachelor. How popular they are at
charity bazaars, and how nice to find that what you bring will certainly sell at the 'bring and buy'.

I find that flowers that are completely dry and full of colour seem to repel dust. Only if they
have faded or lost their colour will they attract and hold dust. For years I have carried out my

Anthony is holding a tray of yellow helychrisums, while
Molly strips and prepares molucella, achillea, old man's
beard, statice and leeks. I am stripping hydrangeas, and am
holding *Hydrangea* 'Hamburg'. In the centre basket are
golden rod, Michaelmas daisy, delphiniums and mullein.

experiments in drying flowers above a very dusty solid fuel Aga, now fondly known as the 'dried flower experimental station', and I am amazed to find that the flowers can hang over it for weeks and still not get dusty.

We have a large arrangement on a pedestal which is still as it was arranged eleven years ago, apart from some of the hydrangeas, which were replaced four years ago. It is quite impossible to dust, but does not seem to need it. It still looks very effective and surprisingly colourful. We are going to keep it, to see for how many years it will give pleasure to us and our friends.

At Stourton House we have a well-established mixed garden with herbaceous borders, woodland areas, artificially made pools and a rockery. We have many mature trees and shrubs and a large vegetable garden. We pick a great many flowers, armfuls of greenery and many seed heads that would, in most gardens, end up as rubbish on the compost heap or bonfire. Nothing is wasted.

We rescue and preserve the unfortunate flowers and tree limbs smashed by storm or snow, and murmur 'It's an ill wind . . .' as we gather each precious piece that we would not normally have dreamed of picking.

The usual concept of dried flowers seems to consist of annuals, statice, helichrysums (or straw flowers), acrocliniums, larkspur and grasses – often dyed! Used on their own as an arrangement, they look stiff and artificial and obviously dried. However, these brightly-coloured flowers are excellent used as highlights among the more subtle colours of dried herbaceous flowers, shrubs and foliage. They then produce an arrangement that looks entirely fresh and straight from the garden.

There are so many flowers and so much greenery, and I mean green, that will dry naturally that you do not need to use chemicals, apart from glycerine for some foliage. You may not have a large garden, but it is very likely that you will find far more in it that will dry than you ever imagined. Your friends and neighbours probably have a lot of different plants, so you can swap flowers with each other. The advantage of dried flowers is that you can go on collecting over a long period, adding to your original arrangement and rearranging it with the newly dried flowers.

Preserving foliage and flowers is an all-year-round process. There is a right time for picking everything and a right way of dealing with it. Obviously the summer and autumn months are the busiest. There is something very satisfying about picking baskets and often barrow-loads of glorious flowers, sitting down to strip off the leaves, then bunching them and finally hanging them up to dry, knowing that they will give pleasure to countless people for years to come when assembled in a gorgeous arrangement.

WHEN TO PICK

For the best colour and result, it is essential to pick your flowers for drying at the correct time. They will not improve in colour once picked, and can often fade and drop if picked a day or so too late, or shrivel if picked too soon.

For instance, a deep pink mophead hydrangea flower will shrivel up and flop if picked when freshly in flower. But if left until the tiny, real flower in the centre of each deep pink sepal has opened and gone over, and the deep pink part of the mophead has changed colour and become set and firm to touch, then it will dry with no trouble. However, while left on the plant, the mophead will go on changing colour, possibly going a deep red or rose pink or mauvey green, according to the amount of light the flower is getting. The final colour of your dried hydrangea will depend entirely on the stage at which you picked that mophead, in other words, on your own decision.

Another example is the blue flower head of echinops, which for the best blue result must be picked just before or as the very first individual florets come out. If left until all are out, the whole head will fall to bits when dry.

Some flowers can be picked and dried perfectly as coloured flowers or, if preferred, can be left until the flower has faded and turned into an interesting seed head. For perfect results with all types of flower, therefore, it is necessary to know the correct picking time and method for drying. The correct time to pick each individual variety

Above: An October basket picked
for drying after the storm of 1987,
including a damaged spray of camellia
foliage, hosta leaves and seed heads,
sedum and *Polygonum amplexicaule*.

Above left: The two largest deep pink Hydrangea mopheads
show the small flowers both in bud and fully out, in the
centre of the pink sepals. These heads will not dry. In the
lower three large mopheads the small flowers are over and
the sepals are changing colour to mauve and deeper pink.
These are now ready to dry.

is indicated in Tables 1, 2 and 3 at the back of the
book.

Obviously it is better to pick your flowers on a
dry day, but if you feel you will miss the best
time to pick a flower it is better to do it in the
rain and shake the raindrops off! It will not be
harmed by doing this.

HOW TO PREPARE

The way in which you prepare your flowers for
drying can make all the difference between
having an arrangement of dried fresh flowers
and one of dried dead ones.

Consider first the way the flower grows naturally – whether the head is erect or hangs down,
whether the stem is stiff and hard, or whether it
will go limp when drying. Is the stem covered in
leaves, and if so are they small and attractive or
will they shrivel and look dead when dry?

Having picked your flowers, prepare them for
drying as soon as possible. Strip the large and
untidy leaves from the stems by holding the
flower head in one hand while sliding the other
hand down the stem. Do not remove very small
green leaves or attractive grey ones. Stiff leaves,

such as those on the stems of eryngiums and
echinops, are beautiful when dry and should
also be kept. They help to keep the flower
looking fresh.

Gather the flowers into small bunches of
approximately ten stems or less, and secure
them with an elastic band twisted several times
round until reasonably tight. The stems shrivel
considerably as they dry, and will fall out of a
slack band. Then hang the bunches at 6-inch
intervals up a piece of string. Use a loose slip
loop for each bunch, so that it tightens as they
dry, and hang the string on a hook or coat-
hanger to dry.

Very heavy or large heads, such as artichokes
or delphiniums, should be tied individually or in

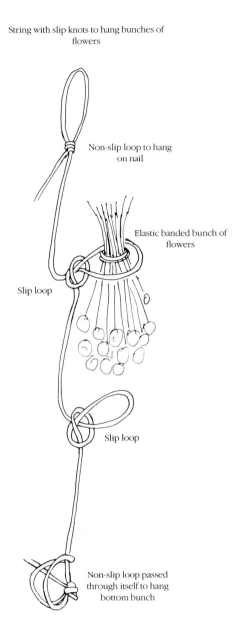

String with slip knots to hang bunches of flowers

Non-slip loop to hang on nail

Elastic banded bunch of flowers

Slip loop

Slip loop

Non-slip loop passed through itself to hang bottom bunch

An early July picture of myself bunching and stringing delphiniums. Hanging on the wall are strings of bunched delphiniums, ammobium and honesty. In the basket are *Alchemilla mollis*, acrocliniums, wheat and wild oats. In the foreground is *Alchemilla mollis* stripped and stood to dry in a cardboard box.

twos, still using a tightly twisted elastic band to prevent the flowers sliding out of the slip knot. Flowers picked wet should be bunched only in very small numbers, to allow plenty of air to circulate around them, otherwise they will go brown.

Flowers with spray or feathery-type heads, such as astilbe, golden rod, alchemilla and arun-

cus, are better dried in an upright position to keep their natural shape. Do not bunch these. Stand them up loosely – an old wine bottle box with partitions left in is an ideal container.

A few flowers or seed heads, for example Chinese lanterns and tree peony seed pods, are best laid flat in a box to dry in order to keep their correct shape.

WHERE TO DRY

Flowers must be dried as quickly as possible in order to ensure that the stems and leaves remain green. Choose a place which is warmed by some artificial means, such as by a water heater, near hot pipes or in an airing cupboard, or even close to an Aga or cooker. Be sure that there is sufficient ventilation for the moisture to escape, and at all costs keep the flowers well away from sunlight or bright daylight – a dark room is best. A warm attic room is a possibility during high summer, provided you black out the window and remember to remove the flowers before the autumn damp spoils them.

Do not try to dry your flowers in a garage, outhouse or loft. And a greenhouse is the worst of all, as it is far too damp and the sun would completely bleach the flowers – unless of course that is what you want!

It is impossible to say how long your flowers will take to dry – so much depends on the variety of flower. For example, grasses take a few days, while sedum takes several months! The temperature of your drying room and the weather outside can make a great difference. It is a good idea, therefore, to be able to recognize when the flowers are really dry.

When properly dried, the flower should feel light and crisp. The whole stem will be stiff and will feel warm, not cold, right up to the head. If you do not wish to use them immediately, seal the flowers away in a black dustbin bag. They can then be stored quite safely in a cold or damp place. Never seal them up on a damp or humid day, as they will come out smelly and mouldy.

DRYING WITH DESICCANTS

Desiccants such as silica gel and borax can be used to dry many flowers that would not dry at all successfully by warm air alone. This method is very useful for small flowers to be used in paperweights or pictures. The disadvantage of this method is that the flowers become very brittle; many take up the damp again on a humid wet day, lose their colour and go limp.

Detailed information on using desiccants is on p. 90.

SUMMARY

1. For successful dried fresh flowers choose good colour and good quality flowers.
2. Pick at the correct time (see the tables on pp. 93–123).
3. Prepare the flowers for drying according to type.
4. Hang, stand or lay them down in a really warm place, well away from too much daylight, until completely dry.
5. Store in airtight conditions until wanted for arranging.

2

PRESERVING FOLIAGE

EVERY FRESH FLOWER arrangement is enhanced by the inclusion of foliage of some sort, and this applies doubly to a dried flower arrangement. Without it, it can look 'dried', with it, it can look 'fresh'.

Foliage can be dried, pressed, ironed or glycerined, according to the material you wish to use and the result you want to achieve.

GLYCERINING

Glycerining is very effective and preserves the foliage for years, keeping it supple and 'live'. It nearly always considerably changes the colour of the leaves.

Refined glycerine can be obtained in small quantities from a chemist but is very expensive. This is the best way to buy it if you wish to dry only a few branches for yourself. Larger quantities of a lower grade can be bought from shops that sell it to farmers, but it is still very costly. However, it is well worth while, especially if you can share the cost between several of you. Anti-freeze is readily obtainable, but it is not very satisfactory to use as it is not possible to know how much glycerine is in it and the colour additive affects the foliage.

First make a mixture using one part of glycerine to two parts of fairly hot water. The simplest way to do this is to place about 1 inch of glycerine in a bottle and add 2 inches of hand-hot water. Shake well to mix and pour into a glass vase or jar. Stand your foliage in the mixture – it is easy to see when the branches have sucked it all up and the vase needs replenishing. Glycerine is so expensive that it is advisable to use only a small quantity at a time.

Place your vase or jar on a non-sunny windowsill or in a light room that is not too hot. Use fresh picked foliage, and cut the stems straight across immediately before standing them in the glycerine. Never strip off the bark. They will drink every drop of the mixture. The vase can be filled with branches and replenished with the mixture if necessary.

Always choose attractively shaped branches with undamaged leaves, picking deciduous foliage from about July onwards until the leaves begin to turn and the sap ceases to rise. Evergreens are best glycerined from autumn to spring, when they are not growing young foliage and dropping old leaves.

How long should the branches be left in the glycerine? It could be a week or two, or much longer. There is no set answer to this but there are several simple ways of deciding when they are ready. First you will see the veins in the leaves changing colour. Then the whole leaf changes colour and the branch ceases to drink the mixture. The time this takes and the colour you finally end up with varies tremendously, depending on the weather, the time of year and where the foliage was growing. For instance, if you pick beech leaves in deep shade you will probably end up with dark green leaves, whereas a branch picked in full sun will probably come out a deep reddish brown.

Some foliage, for example *Elaeagnus ebbingei*, drinks very, very slowly, but after about three months goes a beautiful deep yellow – well worth waiting for!

It is not advisable to leave any foliage in the glycerine after it has turned colour, however, as it will get overdone, sweat and drip the mixture from the leaves, especially in damp weather, and then go mouldy. If this does happen it is possible to wash the branch in a mild mixture of washing-up liquid to remove some of the glycerine. This can also be done if you have had the foliage in an arrangement for several years and it looks a bit dusty!

Store the foliage in a box or an unsealed plastic bag in a dry place until you are ready to use it.

DRYING

At the end of the year the sap ceases to rise in the deciduous trees and shrubs, and then we rejoice for a very short time in the glorious autumn tints in the countryside. By then it is too late to glycerine these leaves, but it *is* the right time to preserve them to keep their brilliant colours.

Beautifully tinted autumn leaves can be dried, by pressing them between blotting paper or by placing sprays under a carpet, a mattress or even under the cushions of an armchair or sofa. Better still for highly coloured leaves such as Virginia creeper or acers, however, is to iron them on blotting paper. Lay the leaf on the blotting paper, set the iron to 'silk', and iron directly on to the leaf until all the moisture has gone and the leaf is like stiff crisp paper. Give them a coating of clear varnish to restore the glossy shine, then wire the leaves on to a branch from their own plant or Sellotape on to a looped wire for arranging.

Let me here issue a warning – do clean the base of your iron before next using it on your best clothes, as it does get very gooey!

SKELETONIZING

Skeletonizing is the rotting away of most of a dead leaf or seed pod until only the tough fibrous part remains in the original shape. This frequently happens naturally in a garden or wood, provided it is reasonably damp and shady and you are not too tidy sweeping up every fallen leaf or seed pod.

You can of course have a skeleton corner in a damp shady place in the garden and make a collection of leaves and seed pods to skeletonize naturally with the help of rain, frost, bacteria and even slugs.

Another method is to put your fallen leaves and/or seed pods into a tub or trough of rain water to allow the bacteria to get to work. This usually takes about three weeks, but could be longer. When the leaves are ready, wash them if necessary and then hang, lay flat or press them to dry.

3
PERENNIAL HERBACEOUS FLOWERS

THERE IS NOTHING difficult and nothing complicated about drying herbaceous flowers. All you need to know is which ones to pick, when to pick them, and how to prepare them. Many of our well-known herbaceous flowers will dry beautifully, as long as they are picked at the correct time and hung or stood in a really warm place well away from too much light. Unfortunately for the proud garden owner, the right time is often when the flowers are full out and looking at their best, and sometimes even before this. However, you can console yourself with the thought that they will last far longer when dried than they would if left in the garden to go to seed or die.

A pedestal arrangement of perennial flowers from the border with shrubs, green foliage and green seed heads. This collection of flowers does not include any annuals specially grown for drying.

1 Hydrangeas	14 Mombretia Leaves
2 Delphiniums	15 Shoo Fly
3 Achillea	16 Glycerined Foliage
4 Paeony	17 Wild Oats
5 Aruncus	18 Carline Thistle
6 Artichoke	19 Golden Rod
7 Centaurea Macrocephala	20 Echinops
8 Eryngium Miss Wilmot's Ghost	21 Double Feverfew
9 Rose Dorothy Perkins	22 Eryngium x Zabelii Jewel
10 Green Lacecap Hydrangea	23 Anaphalis
11 Achillea The Pearl	24 Eucalyptus
12 Honesty	25 Alchemilla Mollis
13 Stachys	26 Michaelmas Daisy

Blue Flowers

Aconitum (blue monkshood)

The blue monkshood is rather similar to a delphinium, and dries well when in full flower, but it must be remembered that it is a very poisonous plant and I do not recommend preserving it.

Catananche

Catananche is supposed to be good for drying, but I find it very unsatisfactory. The blue dandelion-like flowers are so graceful and attractive when growing but insist on closing up when dry, and the best one gets is the silvery calyx with a few blue petals at the end. Usable but disappointing and better dried in a desiccant if you have it. (See hints on p. 90.)

Delphinium

Probably the most striking of all herbaceous dried flowers are the delphiniums, which keep their wonderful colour so well when dried. The picking time for these is crucial. Obviously you want as large and long a flowering spike as possible, but it *must* be picked before the bottom flowers are about to drop. If they have started to drop, two-thirds of the spike of flowers will end as confetti when dry. With good growing weather – not too dry – it is possible to cut and dry perfect heads well over 3 feet long. Cut the spike just below the bottom flower, and leave the side shoots to flower for smaller arrangements.

Hugh raising the string round the clump of *Delphinium* 'Faust' to keep up with its rapid growth. Make a loose cage with thick string round four bamboo canes in order to allow the spikes to sway in the wind and so prevent them snapping off. The well developed delphinium to the right of the centre stick and the one behind Hugh are ready to pick, while the other five spikes need to open a few more buds at the top.

Echinops ritro, showing the centre ball in full flower, which is too late for drying, and the two side flowers in perfect condition.

Hang the spikes upside down in twos or threes, and after a few days, when the individual flowers feel papery and dry, take the spikes down and stand them upright to finish drying. The closed flowers will partially open up again and look more natural.

Here I would like to give a growing hint, as many people tell me they cannot grow delphiniums. They are absolutely hardy plants, but unfortunately they are the favourite food of slugs and snails. In the autumn, to guard against these pests, remove half an inch of soil from the top and round the crown of the plant. Replace this with clean sharp sand, making sure to get it down inside the cut-off hollow stems. Sprinkle a few slug pellets around, and your delphiniums should be bigger and better next spring.

Staking your delphiniums is another very important aid to success. Having succeeded in growing luscious strong spikes, the last thing you want to find is that they have all been blown flat during a wet and windy night. Place four strong, 5-foot bamboo canes, 18 inches apart, round your plant. When the delphinium stems are 12 inches high, tie a string around the four bamboos, beginning and ending on the same stick and only passing the string round the other three. When the stems have grown, slide the string 6 inches up the sticks. As the stems continue to grow, make new circles of string until the flower heads start to develop. The highest string should be 9 inches below the flower head. In this way the delphiniums have sufficient room to sway around in the wind without damaging the flower heads or breaking.

One winter I lost 70 per cent of my very large old delphinium plants. On investigating the remains, I discovered a mouse nest in the middle of each one. 'Where I dines, I sleeps.' I am advised by the leading delphinium growers in this country to split the plants when they become very large, to avoid this happening.

Echinops

To dry echinops like blue balls successfully, the picking time is again all-important. The moment when these are the best shade of blue is when the sun is out and just before the first tiny flowers open. If the head has flowered all over it is a waste of time picking it, as it will shatter into tiny bits when dry.

Echinops ritro is the best blue, and does not become too large a plant. There is another almost navy-blue variety with larger heads, but they are very inclined to fall to bits when they dry, even when picked at the correct time.

Echinops leaves are an attractive shade of grey-green with a silvery reverse side. They dry very well, so do not take them off the stems.

Eryngium

Some of the eryngiums are also a beautiful metallic blue. Like echinops, they must be

Eryngium x 'Zabelii Jewel', showing the correct time for picking, just before all the tiny flowers burst open.

Two baskets loaded with delphiniums and bunches of yellow *Alchemilla mollis* and blue catmint picked for drying from perennial borders.

picked either before or just as the first set of tiny proper flowers come out. They won't fall to bits, but they do lose their blue as soon as they have flowered completely. Don't strip off the leaves. Many varieties dry beautifully. I think the best are the 3-foot tall *Eryngium* x 'Zabelii Jewel', with large blue spiky flowers, and the shorter *Eryngium bourgatii* and *Eryngium alpinum*.

There are several other blue small-flowered varieties, for example *Eryngium tripartitum*.

Nepeta (catmint)

I doubt whether many people would think of drying the common catmint. The larger varieties are much better. Pick it in full flower, while there are plenty of buds still to come out. It dries to a good blue-grey colour.

Yellow and Cream Flowers

Achillea

There are several different varieties of achillea that dry well. The best yellow is 'Gold Plate' with its huge firm heads. A good light yellow variety is

'Moonshine', and there is a large, tall, cream-coloured variety called 'Flowers of Sulphur'. None of these varieties should be picked until each floret has become well developed, with a

Above: Achillea 'Flowers of Sulphur', clearly showing the well-developed 'bobble' stage of the flower, with double feverfew, both ready to pick,

Left: Strippers Doreen and Molly, at work among the ladies' mantle (*Alchemilla mollis*), delphiniums, yellow *Centaurea macrocephala*, a bunch of brown top bent grass and a spray of white *eryngium* (Miss Willmott's ghost).

tiny 'bobble' in the middle, and the whole head feels firm.

Alchemilla mollis (ladies' mantle)

Alchemilla mollis or ladies' mantle is a most useful dried flower that seems to fit into most arrangements. It should be picked when nearly all the tiny acid-yellow flowers are out. Provided the stems are reasonably straight, it can be stood up in a box to dry after being stripped of its largest leaves.

Aruncus (goat's beard)

Aruncus or goat's beard, like a huge 6-foot cream plumed astilbe, must be picked while the main part of the plume is fully out but the tips are still in bud. If the tip is fully out, the whole flower will go brown when dry. It is best dried standing up, to keep its natural shape.

Astilbe

The much shorter and smaller-plumed cream astilbe can be picked when full out as is best, or after flowering as a green seed head. It should also be stood up to dry.

The bright yellow heads of *Centaurea macrocephala* and the cream-flowered phlomis could both have been picked a day or two earlier for best results, but the eryngium is at its best. The lupin will make a good seed head later on.

Centaurea macrocephala

Centaurea macrocephala is an excellent bright yellow flower with large thistle-like heads. It is an early flowerer that can have its leaves left on the stem and be hung up in bunches to dry. Pick when fully out.

Anthony holding an armful of yellow achillea and red love-lies-bleeding while I pick
golden rod. On the trolley are a collection of red and green hydrangeas, pink Michaelmas
daisy, green moluccella, blue delphiniums and purple flowering artichoke, lying on a bed
of golden rod. On the left end of the trolley are green poppy heads, and on the right
green shoo-fly.

Montbretia (crocosmia)

Montbretia or crocosmia can be dried with its
small orange flowers or later at the mature seed
stage. The green strap-like leaves also make a
most useful addition to any dried flower
arrangement. Dry while the stems and foliage
are still green.

Solidago (golden rod)

Golden rod is another very useful flower for
either a large or a small arrangement. It should
be picked when fully out, before the head starts
to turn brown on top. Dry it standing up, but do
not dry in too hot a place as this may cause it to
fall to bits.

White Flowers

White dried fresh flowers, mixed with grey-
leaved materials and blue hydrangeas, make a
beautiful arrangement. Alternatively, white
flowers can be used as highlights in a mixed
collection of other coloured flowers.

Achillea 'The Pearl'

This white pom-pom-flower is excellent to dry. It
will dry pure white if picked when fully out,
before rain or age turns it brown. Bunch and
hang up to dry, leaving the small leaves.

Anaphalis

The various white anaphalis are best picked while most of the papery white flowers are still closed. As they dry they open up. If picked when all the flowers are fully open, the centres of the flowers will drop out when dry. Either way it is still very attractive. Do not strip off the grey leaves.

Three stunningly effective architectural flowers are the Carline thistle with its huge moonlike white flower, *Eryngium giganteum*, with its silver greeny mauve-tinted flowers (often known as 'Miss Willmott's Ghost'), and the silver-leaved thistle-like flowers of the cardoon (*Cynara cardunculus*).

Two small bumble bees gather nectar and pollen from the silver Carline thistle. This flower must not be picked for drying until the stamens turn dark brown.

A head of anaphalis, showing the paper white unopened flowers and the greeny-yellow centres of those that are in full bloom.

Carlina (Carline thistle)

It was evening when I first found Carline thistles growing in the mountains in Austria, where we were caravanning. The next morning, before we hitched up to travel on, I walked into the woods to pick some. They had disappeared. After some puzzled searching, I discovered they had all closed up tight for the night and had not yet opened. They can also be found in Yugoslavia and southern France, where you will often see one used as a 'good luck' decoration in mountain restaurants and bars. They are now a protected flower abroad, so it is necessary to grow

your own for picking. They are not difficult to grow from seed, and sometimes it is even possible to buy growing plants.

Pick the Carline thistle after it has flowered, when the stamens have gone dark brown. When dry, pull them out to reveal the silver centre.

Cynara cardunculus (cardoon)

The cardoon is one of the plants that can be dried as a flower or later as a seed head. It can be dried in full purple flower, or after flowering, when its creamy centre is surrounded by a silvery tipped calyx, or even later still with the calyx removed so that it looks like a huge cream powder puff.

Eryngium giganteum ('Miss Willmott's Ghost')

Eryngium giganteum ('Miss Willmott's Ghost') is a biennial, so you should always leave a few flowers to go to seed. They prefer to grow in a chalky or gravelly soil or between paving stones. The grey spiked leaves are beautifully shaped so should not be removed. Dry them standing upright.

Matricaria eximia (double feverfew)

Another small clustered white flower, similar to *Achillea* 'The Pearl' when dry, is the double feverfew, *Matricaria eximia*. This needs to be

very fully out before picking. Pick sprays of the most fully developed flowers, leaving the remainder to continue growing until ready. Bunch and hang up to dry.

Saxafraga granulata flora plena
This double form of the wild meadow saxifrage, which is now sold in some nurseries, is an excellent white flower for drying. Bunch and hang up to dry.

Eryngium giganteum (Miss Willmott's ghost) should be picked soon after the tiny florets have finished flowering but before the silver flower turns brown.

Grey Flowers

Grey flowers and foliage are a tremendous asset to any arrangement, whether fresh or dry, and look particularly nice when growing with pink or purple flowers in the garden. Only strip off dead brown leaves from grey-leaved plants before drying in bunches or standing up.

Allium porrum (leeks)
I prefer leek flowers to any of the other large grey alliums, as they do not retain their garlicky-onion smell when dry. Some leeks are an attractive pink colour, and they are one of the few flowers that can be hung in a loft or garage to part-dry and lose their smell. Pick them when the maximum number of flowers are out, and as the first seed pods are setting on the top of the heads. Finish drying in a warm place. They make an excellent herbaceous border plant, and if left in the ground after picking they will multiply.

Artemisia
One of the most impressive grey plants is the 3-foot tall *Artemisia ludoviciana*, which has the whitest leaves and stems, but all the artemisias are extremely useful in arrangements. All should be picked when their little flowers are still yellow. Some varieties have a very pungent smell, but *Artemisia ludoviciana* is not unpleasant.

Ballota
Ballota is a lovely small greeny-grey woody plant. It has round clusters of similar coloured 'felt' flowers growing in tiers up the stem. There are two varieties of ballota. It is possible to take the leaves off one and not the other. The only way to discover which is which is by trying the variety you have. They are best dried without bunching, laid flat in a box.

Stachys lanata (lamb's ears)
One of the grey flowers that always comes to mind first is the spiked *Stachys lanata* (lamb's ears) with its mauve flowers. However, there are two other less well-known varieties, both lovely: the first has pure white spikes without the pale

Above: Three sorts of dried stachys. From the left: *Stachys* 'Cottonballs', *Stachys lanata*, which has purple flowers that tend to dry brown, and the white spikes of a non-flowering variety.

Left: Yellow flowered artemisia and blue catmint, ready to pick, but the stachys must develop longer spikes before being picked.

Below: Pink and white leek flower heads being checked before picking.

mauve flowers, and the second has 'bobbles' up the pure white spike and is called 'cottonballs'. All these varieties have lovely felt-like leaves which should be dried lying flat. The flower spikes should be bunched and hung up to dry.

Verbascum and acanthus

The grey verbascums and the green flower spikes of acanthus are tall and stately. Because of their shape, part of the spike will already have gone to seed while the remainder is still flowering. Both are best picked at this stage, so that they remain green when dry.

Pink, Red and Purple Flowers

The herbaceous border will supply some excellent pink, red and purple flowers to add to one's collection. All keep their colour extremely well provided they do not get damp again after being dried. There are, of course, some other very good red or pink flowers and bulbs which will dry only as ripe seed heads. These include hollyhocks, *Lychnis coronaria* with its lovely grey stems and foliage, poppies, tulips and gladioli.

A mass of pink and grey-foliaged plants. Some of these will be dried as flowers, and some will provide architectural seed heads. The former include *Allium sphaerocephalon* (the drumstick allium), cirsium, roses and grey *Stachys lanata*. Poppies, gladioli, hollyhocks and the tall grey spikes of verbascum are used for their seed heads.

Purple heads of cirsium growing near the spiky green leaves of crocosmia. The centre top and the right-hand flowers are ready to pick, the other flowers are under-developed.

The massive flat-headed fluffy flowers of *Eupatorium purpureum* should be picked as seen here, in full flower in late summer.

Achillea

Achillea 'Cerise Queen' and other pink varieties must be left until the colour has slightly faded and each floret has become well developed with a 'bobble' in the middle. It is then ready to pick.

Allium sphaerocephalum

The drumstick allium, *Allium sphaerocephalum*, has a deep red flower. It is grown from a bulb, and is very colourful planted among herbaceous plants and roses. It does unfortunately have to be picked when at its most colourful, just as the first few seed pods set on the top of the seed head.

Astilbe

The 12-inch high bright red astilbe or the taller pink varieites can be dried either at the mature flower stage or as they darken and begin to go over. If left in the garden they are still useful when they have gone brown. Dry them standing up.

Cirsium

Cirsium is a thistle-like purple flower which has no prickles. This can either be dried on its own stem, or the best flowers can be picked off and wired while leaving any buds to develop. Hang or stand to dry. For the best colour, pick the flowers as soon as they come into full bloom.

Eupatorium and Filipendula

The massive, flat-headed, fluffy flowers of *Eupatorium purpureum* and the pink filipendula can both be dried in full flower or as they go over. To dry, hang up the eupatorium and stand the filipendula.

Liatris spicata and Lythrum salicaria

Two excellent purplish-pink spiky flowers are *Liatris spicata* (gay feather) and *Lythrum salicaria* (purple loosestrife). Both should be picked when the maximum number of flowers are out. Hang up to dry.

Michaelmas daisy

Late in the year the old-fashioned flat-topped Michaelmas daisies should be picked when first out and at their best. Do not strip off the leaves. Bunch and hang up to dry. The cerise ones dry a superb colour.

Monarda (bergamot)

Monarda, bergamot, bee balm, or call it what you will, is a flower that does not dry quite as well as one would wish. The small individual flowers twist and shrivel when dry, although they do keep good colour. The red varieties are best, and should be dried when the maximum numbers of flowers are out round the central cushion. Do not remove the leaves – bergamot is a herb, with deliciously scented leaves which keep their scent when dry.

For better drying results use the desiccant method. Cut off the flower head 2 inches below the bottom flower and keep the stem. Insert a fine wire up the flower stalk and bend the wire upwards out of the way. Stand the bergamot flower head in a large clean empty cream or yogurt carton and fill with silica gel crystals until the flower is covered. Leave for a few days till dry. The whorl of flowers will then dry in its correct position. Dry the remaining stem with its leaves on by hanging it upside down. When dry, join the stem and the flower back together again, pushing the wire in the head into the stem.

Nerine

The delicate sugar-pink flowers of the nerine will dry if left in a vase of water until the stems and flowers shrivel. The flowers remain an excellent pink colour. The smaller-flowered varieties are the best to dry.

Paeonia (peony)

The double red or pink peonies are some of the earliest flowers in bloom. They dry very well, although they shrink quite a lot. There are several buds on each stem of a peony, so cut off only the flower that is in full bloom and leave the other buds to develop. Pass a stout stub wire well up into the short cut stem and hang up or stand to dry. Others can be picked with long stems, bunched and hung up to dry. When the flower is nearly dry, smooth out the outer petals over your thumb until the flower regains its original shape. Replace it in the warmth until totally dry.

Should the peony flower be too dry and brittle to handle the petals, breathe on it or hang it in the bathroom while you have a bath. When the petals are pliable, reshape and dry immediately.

The colourful red herbaceous plant bergamot. Pick a few sprays from your border and dry it complete with its leaves, to give a delicious scent to your arrangement.

A colourful corner of the herbaceous border, showing many flowers which can be used for drying. In the left foreground are the pink spikes of *Liatris spicata* with purple lavender, surrounded by the white flowers of the double feverfew. On the right are green poppy seed heads ready to be picked, and in the background is the tall grey *Artemisia ludoviciana* and a yellow lupin which produces a lovely seed head.

September–November, deep red *Polygonum amplexicaule* and frothy pink *Polygonum campanulatum*, make excellent dried flowers. They should all be picked at a length that will suit your arrangement and hung up to dry. The reverse side of the leaves of *Polygonum campanulatum* dries to an interesting coffee colour. *Polygonum affine* is a carpeting variety 12 inches tall. Do not pick until the pink flowers turn red. Dry them standing up.

Polygonum affine, showing freshly flowering pink spikes and the red ones of those that have matured and are now ready to pick for drying. Among the polygonum is the yellow Welsh poppy, providing attractively shaped small seed heads. The pink lupin will develop into spikes of long pea-like pods covered in silky grey hairs. To the right of the path are *Hosta sieboldiana* flowers which will be dried as seed heads; the leaves will be picked for drying just before they turn yellow.

Polygonum

Polygonum bistorta 'Superbum', which produces 2-foot pale pink spikes in May, and two taller varieties flowering in the period

Sedum 'Autumn Joy'

In October *Sedum* 'Autumn Joy' will have matured to a deep autumn red. This will be the best time to pick the flower heads. The fleshy stems will take months to dry properly. Strip the leaves off the stalks and hang in bunches in the warmest possible place. If they are to be used immediately in an arrangement it doesn't matter if the stems are still a little damp. However, don't store them damp or they will go mouldy.

Filling-in Flowers

When arranging a vase or bowl of flowers there always seems to come a time when it is necessary to cover the Oasis or wire and fill in the gaps between the flowers. *Alchemilla mollis* and golden rod have already been mentioned. These are two very useful 'fillers-in' for yellow-tinged arrangements. But for pink or white colour schemes the perennial statice or dainty gypsophila would be more suitable.

Gypsophila

There are several different sorts of gypsophila. One kind has very fine tiny white flowers and is sometimes known as baby's breath. Another has slightly larger flowers and comes with single or double pink or white flowers. Pick sprays of the most well-developed flowers and dry in a warm place, well away from daylight, thus keeping the stems green. *Gypsophila* 'Bristol Fairy' is an excellent double white variety that can be saved and dried from a bouquet of bought flowers.

Statice dumosa (sea lavender) and Statice latifolia

Statice dumosa or sea lavender, which has white flowers and is found growing wild on some beaches, and *Statice latifolia* with smaller lilac-coloured flowers, should both be picked when the maximum number of flowers are out. Either hang up or stand to dry.

Thalictrum

If you are lucky enough to have a large hazy clump of the mauve thalictrum you may feel able to spare some to dry. This keeps its colour for only a few months but forms good tall 'filler-in' material for very large arrangements. Dry it standing up to keep its shape.

Double Flowers

You will find that various double flowers can be dried with great success by just bunching or hanging separately in a really warm place. The double yellow heliopsis is one of these, and yellow or orange marigolds, pom-pom or small decorative dahlias and chrysanthemums are others. They also respond very well to drying in a desiccant.

Chrysanthemums

Sprays of small round double pom-pom chrysanthemums make excellent dried flowers. Bunch the sprays and hang them in a warm place to dry. The very double decorative type will also dry in the same way. The clearer the colours the better.

Dahlias

Choose strong-coloured but not too dark pom-pom or medium size very double decorative dahlias for drying. Pick as soon as they are full out, and well before they show signs of dropping. Make small bunches of three or four flowers, or wire individually by passing a stub wire up a short piece of stem into the flower head. Hang over a string or coat-hanger in a very warm place. Excellent results are produced by burying in a desiccant.

Others

Gnaphalium and Leontopodium alpinum (edelweiss)

Two rockery plants which dry well are gnaphalium, with clusters of tiny yellow everlasting flowers, and edelweiss, *Lontopodium alpinum*. Bunch and hang the gnaphalium, but lay the edelweiss flat to dry.

Helleborus

The white Christmas rose, *Helleborus niger*, and the white, pink and dark red Lenten rose, *Helleborus orientalis*, which flowers from February onwards, unfortunately do not dry satisfactorily by warm air alone. This is surprising, as they look as if they should when they begin to turn green. However, it is possible to dry them all in a desiccant when the flowers have just set seed. The flowers tend to be rather floppy after drying, so split the sprays into small sprigs after picking and pass a very fine stub wire right up the stem to stiffen it before drying.

There are many more perennial border plants that might well be good subjects for drying, so do some experimenting, especially with plants that have very double flowers.

There is nothing very difficult about drying

Helleborus orientalis, the Lenten rose, looks as if it should
dry very easily when it begins to turn green. However, this is
not the case, and it is necessary to dry by a desiccant method.

fleshy flowers such as large French marigolds
and roses provided the drying temperature is
high enough. A plate warming oven in a solid
fuel cooker is ideal. Leave the oven door slightly
open to allow moisture to escape and to prevent
flowers cooking!

Remember:

1. Pick the flowers at the correct time (see the
tables at the back of the book).
2. Prepare them carefully for drying.
3. Dry them in a very warm and if possible dark
place.
4. Leave them until completely dry before stor-
ing or arranging.

4
ANNUALS AND BIENNIALS

S O FAR I HAVE talked mostly about perennial plants which continue to grow and flower year by year, but there is a very important category for drying that needs to be planted every year – annuals and biennials. I look upon these flowers as the highlights in a flower arrangement, as they are usually more brightly coloured than the perennials.

Some can be seeded direct into the ground, while others are best started in the greenhouse or indoors, pricked out into boxes of compost when large enough, and finally, when the weather is warm enough, planted into the garden. These annuals, planted between your perennials or along the front of your shrub border, can add considerably to the colour and interest of your garden. It is possible to get packets of separate colours of some annuals if you wish for special colour schemes, but the mixed packets are usually very good.

Plants best started indoors or in a greenhouse are: acrocliniums, amaranthus (Green Thumb), ammobium, helichrysum, moluccella (bells of Ireland), rhodanthe, *Statice sinuata* and *Statice Suworowi* ('pink pokers'). Prick them out into boxes of compost before finally planting them out in the garden.

Annuals which can be sown direct into the ground include: amaranthus (love-lies-bleeding and 'Princes' Feather'), calendula (marigold), candytuft, clarkia, clary, cornflowers, larkspur, lonas, nicandra (shoo-fly), nigella (love-in-a-mist), poppy and xeranthemum.

An easy way to see what all these annual flowers look like is to look in a seed catalogue or on the seed packets in a garden centre.

As with the perennials, it is vitally important that they are picked at the correct stage of their development.

FLOWERS TO BE PICKED WHEN FULLY OUT

The daisy-like, long stemmed pink or white acrocliniums, double orange calendula (marigold), many-coloured double clarkia, clary, mixed coloured double cornflowers, yellow clustered lonas, sky-blue nigella and rose and purple xeranthemum should all be picked when full out, bunched tight with elastic bands and hung upside down on a string to dry in warmth.

Opposite: A basket of annuals including purple larkspur, many-coloured helichrysums, pink and white yellow-centred acrocliniums, green poppy seed heads, white double feverfew, yellow-centred white ammobium and a green spike of *Amaranthus* 'Green Thumb' and black shoo-fly.

The long red ropes of love-lies-bleeding must be picked when the seed has set and they feel thick and firm. Beside them are the splitting seed pods of *Paeonia delavayii*, a tree peony.

Acroclinium

Acrocliniums have 12-inch stems bearing daisy-like flowers in shades of pink or white, with yellow or occasionally black centres. These dry well on their own stems but tend to flop on a humid day. Bunch and hang them in a warm place. Alternatively, cut off the flower heads leaving ½ inch of stem and pass a stub wire up this into the head. Stand them in a jar to dry. They make excellent bright spots in an arrangement.

Amaranthus (love-lies-bleeding)

The amaranthus family, whether the magnificent red or green ropes of love-lies-bleeding, the stately red plumes of 'Princes' Feather', the short red spikes of 'Pigmy Torch' or the unusual short green spikes of 'Green Thumb', must be left to grow until they cease to produce their tiny yellow flecks of stamens. They should be allowed just to set seed and should feel really firm to the touch. If picked too early they shrivel to thin strings! Don't pick the whole plant at once – leave the side shoots to grow.

Pick the main rope of love-lies-bleeding behind the bend, and hang to dry hitched over a string or coat-hanger. 'Pigmy Torch' and 'Green Thumb' have very little stem, so push a stub wire

up the stem before drying. This helps when arranging.

Clarkia elegans

An annual that makes good dried flowers is the most double variety of *Clarkia elegans*, with its tall spikes of strongly coloured carnation-like flowers. Either bunch and hang or stand up to dry.

Cornflower and nigella (love-in-a-mist)

Cornflowers and nigella (love-in-a-mist) are two blue flowers suitable for the smaller arrangement. Dark blue cornflowers are the most effective, but other colours can also be dried. The more double the flowers are the better, and both should be picked immediately they are fully out. Nigella produces a really beautiful seed head.

A collection of annuals that could be sown directly outdoors. Dark blue double cornflowers, light blue love-in-the-mist with decorative seed pods, pink acrocliniums and rhodanthe.

Lonas annua and Helichrysum subulifolium

Lonas annua is a multi-headed bright yellow flower that dries well, and there is a new single bright yellow *Helichrysum subulifolium*. These should both be bunched and hung to dry.

Salvia horminum (clary)

Clary has spikes of brightly-coloured, veined, white, pink or mauve leafy branches. The leaves are really 'bracts', and provided they do not grow too lush in a wet summer they dry extremely well. They should not be picked until they feel firm and wiry.

Statice sinuata

The familiar brightly-coloured dried flower *Statice sinuata* can now be found in individual colours and mixed shades, which include some very attractive pinks and apricots. This plant loves growing in limy soil, and must not be picked until the clusters of flowers are all fully out. Bunch and hang up immediately in a warm place in order to keep the stems green and looking fresh. In a really bad, wet summer the heads of *Statice sinuata* will not develop properly before damping off.

BEDDING PLANTS

Another group of annuals are those which are usually used as bedding plants and must be started off in the greenhouse. Ageratum, asters, celosia (cockscomb), African or French marigolds, *Salvia splendens*, stocks and zinnias all dry well when fully out. Where relevant, choose a medium-sized or large but very double-flowered variety, as they shrink considerably when dried.

These annuals can either be picked, bunched and hung to dry in a very warm place, or have their heads wired like helichrysums and acrocliniums. Fleshy heads often dry best when wired. This is done by leaving ½ inch of stem below the heads and pushing a florist's 'stub' wire up the stalk into the head of the flower, being careful not to push it right through. Stand the wired flowers in a jam jar to dry, or hang by the wires over a tight line.

FLOWERS TO BE PICKED BEFORE FULLY OUT

Ammobium

The small white-flowered sprays of ammobium should be picked when the first few flowers show their yellow centres and the largest buds are all white. If you leave them until all the flowers have come out, they go black in the centre and misshapen. Picked at the correct time, they remain pure white when dry. Leave the small developing shoots to grow into more flowers for future picking.

Helichrysum

Helichrysum seed can now be bought in mixed or individual colours – yellow, white, pink, apricot, orange, and a startling red variety called 'Hot Bikini'. These straw flowers, as they used to be called in the old days, are much improved in

Helichrysum 'Hot Bikini', a 12-inch high startling red variety.

The annual bells of Ireland (*Moluccella laevis*), showing the bells with the flower in bud,
the bells with the flowers opened up, and at the top of the picture the bells which have
dropped their flowers, at which stage they are ready to pick. This spike was picked too
early to be of any real use either dried or glycerined. The wild clematis (old man's beard)
is shown ready to be glycerined. The curly bits should be short and firm, and the seeds
should be half-developed and have a reddish tinge.

quality, but it is still vitally important to pick them at the right time and dry them correctly to get perfect results.

Always pick helichrysum flowers before they have fully opened up. If picked when open, the petals will all turn backwards as they dry, leaving a very ugly-looking bloom. Pick the main flower of each spray, keeping ½ inch of stem. Then push a stub wire up the stem, just into the head. Be careful not to push too far, or the wire will show when the flower dries and opens up. After removing the main flower, the side buds will develop into large flowers with long stems. These can either be cut and wired or dried on their own stems. The stems shrink considerably as they dry, so bunch them tightly and hang them in a warm place. The wired heads can be stood in a jar, where they will start to open up immediately, like magic!

Larkspur (annual delphinium)

Larkspur, or the annual delphinium as it is sometimes listed in seed catalogues, is a tall, elegant, spiky plant with excellent clear shades of red, pink, lilac, mauve and white flowers. It is a 'must' for a fresh or dried flower arrangement.

Pick the larkspur spray down to the next

young shoot and you will be able to continue picking all summer. The flower spray must be picked before the bottom flowers begin to drop.

Moluccella (bells of Ireland)

Moluccella (bells of Ireland) is not easy to grow. The seed must be germinated at a temperature of 70°F, and the plant needs plenty of moisture to grow in summer, and a dry autumn to flower and leave its beautiful green-veined bell-shaped calyx to mature and not rot. Pick it when the tiny white flowers have gone over and the 'bells' are firm and papery but still green. Strip off the leaves and hang in the dark to keep them green. After drying handle with care, as they are very brittle.

If glycerined, moluccella stays pliable, but will turn a light beige or almost white if left in the sun.

Rhodanthe

Rhodanthe has daisy-like flowers of shocking pink or white, with delightful nodding buds, and grows to only 9 inches tall. For best effect, pick the sprays with large buds when the first flowers open and leave the rest of the plant to grow on for later picking. Some of the buds will open as they dry. The others look enchanting, still closed. Bunch and hang up to dry.

Statice suworowii (pink pokers)

Statice suworowii, often called pink pokers, has tall mauvey-pink spikes of flowers. Before picking, allow the spikes to grow as tall as possible without the bottom flowers going over.

Kochia (burning bush)

Kochia is a compact plant that turns red. Pick the whole plant when a good colour and hang to dry in a very warm place.

ANNUALS FOR SEED HEADS

Candytuft, nicandra, nigella and poppy are all grown for their seed heads. Where possible, pick them while still green.

There are other annuals or bedding plants that will dry in some form or other, so don't hesitate to try a bit of experimental drying for the fun of it. (See p. 56 for more on seed heads.)

SUMMARY

1. Sow annuals early.
2. Pick the flowers at the correct time (see the tables on p.107).
3. Prepare, bunch or wire immediately.

4. Dry in a really warm place until completely dry.
5. Store airtight until wanted for arranging.

5

FLOWERING SHRUBS

SHRUBS ARE ANOTHER useful source of flowers for drying, and can be found and picked all the year round.

WINTER-FLOWERING SHRUBS

Some of the winter- or very early spring-flowering shrubs are well worth drying. Don't throw away your vase of witch hazel or mimosa branches when they are over – they will still look nice in a dried flower arrangement when dried.

Corylopsis pauciflora and Prunus subhirtella autumnalis

The dainty, creamy-yellow-flowered *Corylopsis pauciflora* and the pale pink tiny-flowered *Prunus subhirtella autumnalis* or winter flowering cherry are two more shrubs to be enjoyed first in a vase and then dried as they go over. Either leave to continue drying in the vase, or remove and finish in a warm place.

Hamamelis mollis (witch hazel)

The beautifully scented *Hamamelis mollis* or witch hazel can be picked and dried direct from the bush for best colour, but less shrivelling takes place if it is left in a vase with a little water until it dries.

Jasminum nudiflorum

The yellow winter-flowering *Jasminum nudiflorum* dries excellently. It will look its best if picked when the first flowers are open and the rest of the buds just bursting.

Mimosa

Mimosa usually comes from a florist or in that surprise presentation bouquet of fresh flowers in late winter or early spring. If you live in the southern part of England you can probably grow your own, either outside or in a cold greenhouse or conservatory. When it is fully out, hang the sprays up or leave them in water until dry. Glycerine the foliage, then join the flowers and foliage back together again.

EARLY SPRING SHRUBS

Double pink cherry

Pick small sprays of the candyfloss-pink double cherry before the wind has time to blow the petals away. Pick it as it comes out, while some of the flowers are half open. Dry very warm.

Erica and calluna (heather)

Ericas and callunas (heathers), flowering from the autumn through the winter into the spring, make excellent dried flowers. They should be picked when the lower flowers of the raceme

Above: The delicate cream flowers of *Corylopsis pauciflora* herald the beginning of spring and the end of winter. These dry beautifully.

Right: Pick small sprays of the candyfloss-pink double cherry before the wind has time to blow the petals away. It is best to pick it as it comes out, with some flowers half open. Dry very warm.

are open and the top ones still in bud. Do not dry in too hot a place for too long, or the leaves and flowers will crumble away.

Kerria

Later in the spring the double kerria makes a lovely splash of deep orangey yellow. Choose the sprays with the most flowers, and trim off any unflowering twigs. Bunch and hang up to dry.

Phlomis (Jerusalem sage)

The yellow flowers of the grey-leaved phlomis are best picked when half through their flowering cycle. However, they make good green seed heads if you miss the flowers. Do not strip off the leaves – bunch and hang up. (This plant can cause some people to have hay-fever.)

Syringa (lilac)
Surprisingly, the double-flowered syringa or lilac dries and keeps its scent. The darker colours are best. Remove unflowering twigs and all the leaves, and hang in a very warm place.

The deep yellow double blooms of kerria, ready to pick. These make excellent dried flowers and keep their colour perfectly.

SUMMER-FLOWERING SHRUBS

Buddleia
The yellow spikes of *Buddleia* 'Golden Glow' or *Buddleia weyeriana*, the lilac flowers of *Buddleia crispa* and the dark violet flowers of *Buddleia* 'Black Knight' retain their delicious scent when dried.

Caryopteris and ballota
The blue-flowered caryopteris and the greeny-grey ballota are two useful small shrubs. The grey leaves can either be left on or picked off the ballota. Dry them flat, in a box.

Cytisus (broom)
Some of the brooms, such as the very small-flowered cream variety, make delightful dried flowers to add lightness and brightness to an arrangement. Pick the sprays when they are nearly in full flower, and hang to dry in the warm. Some varieties are available as early as the beginning of May. The flowers shrivel a bit when dry, but keep perfect colour.

The yellow *Cytisus battandieri*, or pineapple-scented broom, is a lovely scented summer-flowering shrub. Do not remove the grey leaves as they look attractive when dried. Pick when fully out and dry quickly.

Hydrangeas
See next chapter, p. 47.

Dried ballota, with most of its leaves removed.

The flowers of broom are best picked when just fully out.

Lavender

Scented sprays of lavender were probably one of the first flowers ever to be dried, and it is usually thought of mainly as an ingredient for pot-pourri. However, both the flowers and the grey foliage are very pleasant in a dried arrangement.

Philadelphus and deutzia

Double-flowered varieties of philadelphus (mock orange) and deutzia should be picked when fully out but before they begin to drop. Remove any unnecessary twigs and strip off all the leaves. Hang in bunches to dry.

Rose

Very few gardens are without that most glorious summer flower, the rose – whether a luxuriant country garden or a cosy walled village garden, a tiny overlooked city backyard or the garden of a brand new house.

A great many roses dry very well, so try out those you have. You will have most success with medium- to large-sized double roses, with strong coloured but not too dark flowers. Roses tend to shrink and darken as they dry. They should be picked when in half to three-quarters open bud, and dried on their own stems. Alternatively, cut off the flower leaving ½ inch of stem and push a wire up it, into the hip. Stand or hang up to dry. Never pick fully blown roses – they always fall to bits and are then fit only for pot-pourri. Dry in a really warm place. Drying roses by warm air alone causes them to shrink a lot. Drying by using the desiccant method avoids a lot of shrinkage, but the flowers are much more brittle and tend to flop on a damp day.

Roses. In the centre is a fresh rose. The two roses on the left
have been wired and air dried, while the two on the right
have been wired and dried in silica gel.

You can now buy special roses, called 'Gar-nette' roses, to grow for drying. As they tend to dry a darker colour, it is best to choose mid-coloured flowers for drying. The pillar rose 'Dorothy Perkins', in either its pink or its red form, is a superb flower for drying. The huge sprays of small double pink flowers should be left until all the buds are out. This will mean that all the earlier flowers will have fallen off. Pick off the thorns and leaves, bunch in twos to fours, and hang them up to dry in the dark and warmth. Should the weather be very damp, shake all the moisture off each spray and hang in the warmest place possible.

Rosemary
Rosemary is a shrubby herb with good greeny-grey foliage and an enjoyable perfume. Cut sprays and hang up to dry.

Santolina and Helichrysum serotinum
The santolinas and the curry-scented *Helichrysum serotinum* have grey foliage and yellow flowers that dry well.

Spiraea
Flowering continuously throughout the summer and autumn are the pink fluffy spikes of the 6-foot tall *Spiraea douglasii*, another useful shrub for drying when fully out. Keep the leaves on, bunch, and hang to dry.

The shrubs listed above will definitely dry well, but there are probably many more that are worth experimenting with.

Hydrangeas are undoubtedly the best flowering shrub for drying, and they are dealt with in detail in the next chapter.

6
HYDRANGEAS

WHAT WOULD I DO without hydrangeas! I consider them to be the best value flower of all for drying. They provide so much wonderful colour in an arrangement – pink, blue, red, mauve and the always useful shades of green. Sadly many people who garden on very limy soil will have difficulty in growing them except in tubs: however, you may have a friend who grows them and will let you have some to dry.

In order to dry hydrangeas successfully it is a help to know a bit about them. They like best to grow in a moisture-retaining acid or neutral soil. They like semi-shade, or to have their roots shaded if in full sun. There are a great many different varieties of hydrangea, and basically there

The mophead hydrangea 'Altona' in varying stages of development. The top right and left flower heads with the white-centre sepals are too immature even to last in water. The mauve head has just finished flowering and the pink head is still flowering; neither will dry. Those which are red tinged green or blue or purple with green are all ready to dry.

are three main shapes of flower head – lacecap, bun-shaped mopheads, or conical flower heads.

The colour of a hydrangea growing in your garden depends on the degree of lime or acid in your soil. Pale pink flowers will turn to pale blue in acid soil, while deep pink will change to deep blue and will be a stunning mauve or purple for several years while they change.

The large coloured individual florets of a hydrangea head are sepals and are sterile. The real flower is small and inconspicuous, in the centre of each sepal. It opens to show attractive stamens when the head has been in colour for a few weeks.

Many varieties have flowers that dry very well. Some will dry sometimes, but a few will never dry satisfactorily. Hydrangea heads will not dry when freshly flowering. They will not even last as a cut flower in water until the real flowers are all out, and, in order to dry, the real flower must be over and gone. The whole head has then to mature, 'turn colour' and feel firm and papery before it is ready to dry.

THE BEST HYDRANGEA VARIETIES FOR DRYING

'Altona', 'Europa and 'Hamburg'
The deep pink or blue hydrangeas – 'Altona', 'Europa' or 'Hamburg' – will turn from faded pink to olive green in shade and to bright red in full sun when ready to dry. On acid soil the deep blue flowers turn to purple/navy blue.

'Blue Wave'
The blue lacecap 'Blue Wave' (which confusingly is often pink on neutral to limy soil) sometimes goes a lovely bluey or pinky grey, magenta or purple if left on the bush long enough, provided the frosts don't come too soon. They are then ready to dry. Lay flat in a box after removing leaves.

'Frillybet'
A delightful branch sport of 'Mme Moullière', the hydrangea 'Frillybet' has very pale blue or pink flowers and dries a delicate shade of duck-egg blue or lime green. It has attractive notched edges to the sepals.

'Générale Vicomtesse de Vibraye'
One of the best and easiest hydrangeas to dry is the pale pink or blue 'Générale Vicom-

Hydrangea 'Blue Wave', showing the fertile flowers in the centre of the blue and pink lacecap heads which are not ready to dry. This lacecap will not dry until the fertile flowers have gone over and the pink or blue sepals have turned to the greeny mauve stage.

tesse de Vibraye'. The mop-head flowers will not be ready to pick until they have changed colour. If pink they will go lime green in the shade or fade to creamy pink in sun. If blue they will turn to bluey green in shade and deeper blue, some-times touched with purple, in full sun. They will then be ready to dry.

'Mme Moullière'

When ready to dry, the white hydrangea 'Mme Moullière' goes a wonderful lime green in shade or a faded white flecked with crimson in full sun.

H. paniculata grandiflora

Hydrangea paniculata grandiflora develops an attractive pink tinge to its parchment-coloured flowers when it is ready to dry. Unfortunately this colour does not last long after drying, and the flower soon turns to beige on a damp day.

'Preziosa' and 'Grayswood'

Two other exciting hydrangeas to grow for drying are the mophead 'Preziosa' and the lacecap 'Grayswood'. Both have super red or purple-tinted flowers as they mature.

'Soeur Thérèse'

'Soeur Thérèse' is another white variety that turns green strongly tinged with red when ready to dry.

Hydrangea 'Veitchii', a white lacecap. The flower head on the right shows the freshly flowering fertile flowers and the white sepals. The left-hand flower shows the white sepals turning green and the fertile flowers nearly over, at which point the lacecap will be ready to pick for drying.

'Veitchii'

White lacecaps also go a pure lime green in the shade when ready to dry. The best variety, 'Veitchii', when grown in half shade, has lime green flowers at the back of the bush and green overtoned in pink or mauve on the top and front of the bush where the sun touches them.

H. villosa

Hydrangea villosa has a pinky mauve lacecap flower head. It will not dry until the centre fertile flowers have set seed and turned a dark reddish brown and the outer florets have turned plum colour. Lay flat in a box to dry.

DRYING HYDRANGEAS

An easy way to tell if a hydrangea head is really ready to pick for drying is to part the top florets and make sure there are not a lot of fresh soft flowers under the top 'turned' ones. These soft florets would shrivel and turn brown instead of drying.

Strip off the leaves and remove any brown florets or pieces from the flower, then bunch and hang them up in a warm and if possible dark place. They will take 2–3 weeks to dry completely, including the stalk.

Dry hydrangeas will very quickly lose their colour and fade if arranged in direct sunlight, and they will turn brown if they are allowed to get damp.

If for some reason or other you have to pick your hydrangea flowers before they are really ready to dry, it may be possible to 'finish' them by putting them into water and leaving them until they either dry or die!

Hydrangea flowers must be picked before the frosts come. They will go brown overnight as soon as they are frosted.

A deep blue mophead hydrangea, 'Hamburg', which has turned to purple on the surface but still has some fleshy petals underneath and will therefore need a few more days before picking.

Myself with a trolley of hydrangeas ready to dry in late autumn.

SUMMARY

1. Do not pick until flowers have 'turned' – blue to blue/green, pink to lime green, deep pink to greeny pink or bright red, purple to deep purple, white to green.
2. Check that the inner petals have 'turned'.
3. They must be dried quickly in good warmth in a dim/dark room.
4. Store or arrange them in a dry place away from direct sunlight.

7

SCENTED FLOWERS AND HERBS

SOME OF THE flowers already mentioned under other headings have an added attraction – a lovely scent which stays with them after drying. Flowers such as roses, peonies, bergamot, marigold, lavender, scented chamomile and lemon balm are regular ingredients of pot-pourri. These will dry on their own stems sufficiently well to be useful as a scented or aromatic addition to an arrangement. Other herbs may not keep such a delicious fragrance, but dry well and are very useful visually.

Scented lilies and poppies which will make good seed heads,
scented roses, catmint, yellow *Alchemilla mollis* and grey
stachys ready for picking on this warm summer's day.

SHRUBS WHICH RETAIN THEIR SCENT WHEN DRIED

Balsam poplar

Glycerined branches of balsam poplar leaves smell quite delicious, and the scent lingers on quite strongly for years. The leaves go a lovely medium brown colour on the upper side and a lighter suede colour on the reverse side.

Buddleia

Buddleia weyerana 'Golden Glow' and *B. crispa* are nicely scented, but *B.* 'Black Knight' has the strongest perfume of all. Pick them in full flower – if possible when the sun is warming them and drawing out their fragrance. Remove any very large leaves and hang them up to dry.

Cytisus battandieri

In midsummer *Cytisus battandieri*, the pineapple-scented broom, will dry very well when fully out, remaining yellow and keeping its scent. Pick the flowers with short stalks and hang up to dry.

Hamamelis mollis (witch hazel)

The scented winter-flowering witch hazel, *Hamamelis mollis*, can either be hung to dry immediately it is picked or left in a vase of water to scent the room until it dries naturally. Unfortunately it does not retain very much of its perfume.

Hyssop and rosemary

Hyssop and rosemary can be dried either when flowering or as sprays of green foliage, and will keep their scent.

Lavender, Helichrysum serotinum, and santolina

The blue-flowered lavender, the yellow-flowered, curry-scented *Helichrysum serotinum*, with grey foliage, and the yellow-flowered santolina, also with grey foliage, are all low-growing aromatic shrubs which produce flowers that can be dried separately from their foliage. Sprays of the foliage will also make excellent filler-in or background flower-arranging material. All should be bunched and hung up to dry.

Lilac and philadelphus

Two spring-flowering shrubs that keep their scent when dried are the double-flowered lilac and the double-flowered philadelphus 'Virginal'. The dark-coloured double lilacs are best, and being very fleshy need plenty of heat to dry them quickly. Pick when their fragrance is strongest.

Marjoram

The pink-flowered marjoram has sprays of flowers that can be dried separately from or together with its green foliage. Both the flowers and the foliage keep their scent.

Roses and peonies

Roses, particularly the old-fashioned ones, and double peonies have delicious scents. The ideal time to pick them in order to keep the fragrance and yet have a good dried flower is when the rose is three-quarters out and the peony just fully out, at noon on a warm sunny day. The sun draws out the scent of flowers, so they need to be hung in a warm place to dry immediately while they are still warm from the sun.

HERBS WITH SCENTED FLOWERS AND FOLIAGE

Artemisia and tarragon

The grey artemisias and the green-leaved cooking herb tarragon grow into tall spiky sprays and should be picked as they produce their tiny

A circular herb bed, home for purple chives, calamintha, tarragon, foxglove, lemon balm, orris and, in the centre, large-leaved garlic mustard and green and purple honesty.

yellow flowers. Hang or stand to dry. (A few artemisias have a very pungent smell which may be offensive to some people.)

Basil
Basil is a deliciously scented herb that produces very attractive spikes of seed heads in the late summer. This is only a tender annual, and needs a warm summer to succeed.

Bergamot
The red-flowered bergamot has deliciously scented foliage and a striking wheel-like flower. This can be hung up to dry complete with leaves. The flowers, although remaining red, become very misshapen – for better results, dry in silica gel. (See p. 90 for details.)

Calendula (marigolds)
Dried marigolds keep a little of their aromatic perfume. Either dry on their own stems, or pick the heads and pass a fine florist's wire up ½ inch of stem into the head and hang up to dry.

Chives
The mauve-flowered chives lose their onion smell when dried. It is advisable to put a florist's wire up the hollow stem of each flower before standing them in a jar to dry.

Lemon balm
Lemon balm should be picked when the long branching spikes of seed heads are well developed but still green. Strip off the large untidy leaves, but dry the small ones.

Meadowsweet and chamomile

The cream-plumed meadowsweet and the tiny daisy-flowered chamomile called the scented mayweed are both wild flowers. Both are lovely to dry for their scent, but chamomile shrivels considerably and looks a little untidy. Hang up to dry.

Mint

Apple mint, wild mint and all the other mints with their mauve flowers and scented foliage are both decorative and delicious additions to an arrangement. They all have very different perfumes. Pick when the flowers have become a long spike.

Nepeta (catmint)

Nepeta, the catmint, makes an excellent dried flower if picked complete with foliage when in full flower. If you possess a cat, it is advisable not to use catmint in an arrangement. Your cat will have an uncontrollable desire to eat it or sit in the middle of it.

Parsley

Curled parsley makes a good green filler-in material for an arrangement. Pick during the autumn, winter or spring, when mature and firm, and dry in bunches. (It can even be picked from your dried flower arrangement when needed for cooking.)

Stocks

Highly scented double-flowered stocks need to be dried in a very warm place. Bunch in pairs or threes and hang up to dry.

Sweet cicely

Sweet cicely has lovely clusters of black boat-shaped seed pods, which should be picked while still green to prevent them dropping off. The delicate aniseed-scented leaves are best pressed or dried flat. This is myrrh, the plant often mentioned in the Bible, and it can be used by diabetics to sweeten food.

Tansy

Tansy is a rather unpleasantly strong-smelling herb, but it has very good clustered heads of yellow button-like flowers. These will also dry well when they have turned black. Luckily it loses most of its smell when dry.

Most scented herbs should be bunched and hung up to dry, and of course their leaves should be kept on. Always dry them in a warm place, otherwise they are likely to go brown. Just a few of these perfumed flowers, mixed into an arrangement, will scent the whole house.

Two herbs which do not have scented flowers but look good dried are *Alchemilla mollis* and *Polygonum bistorta*, which are described in more detail in the chapter on perennials.

OPPOSITE
Above: The deliciously fragrant small-flowered scented mayweed, growing in a dense patch in a corner of a cornfield.

Below: The long boat-shaped seed pods of sweet cicely (*Myrrhis odorata*) should be picked just before they go black.

8

SEED HEADS

To OBTAIN A REALLY wonderful arrangement of dried flowers in your home, you are bound to depend largely on drying fresh summer flowers. But some seed heads, such as Chinese lanterns and stinking iris, can be extremely colourful, while others have shapes which are architecturally most interesting.

Imagine for a moment that you are picking a collection of midsummer flowers from your garden for a fresh arrangement. There would be no ripe seed heads. On the other hand, there would be quite a few which were green and which you would consider an excellent addition to your fresh arrangement.

GREEN SEED HEADS

Plan ahead, and pick these seed heads specially for drying, while they are still green. Aquilegia, candytuft, delphinium, foxglove, honesty, Jacob's ladder, love-in-a-mist, poppy, shoo-fly, sweet rocket and teasel are all good picked green, but be sure that the seed pods are well developed before you pick them, otherwise they will shrivel when dry.

Sweet rocket and honesty

Two contrasting types of green seed head are sweet rocket and honesty. Sweet rocket has 4- to 5-inch long thin pods, and honesty has round, flat 'pennies'. Picked green or purple, honesty can be used either as it is when dry, or, providing the seeds are well developed, can have the outer bits of the pods stripped off to reveal the shining green 'pennies' inside. Both should be stripped of large leaves, but the small or fine leaves should be retained. Bunch and hang in a warm, dark place, then they will remain green or purple.

Add these green seed heads to your dried fresh summer flowers and the summer effect will last indefinitely. Here I offer one word of warning – the green will fade to beige if you put them too near a sunny window.

Later in the year there will be many brown or beige seed heads which will give an identical summer flower collection an autumn feeling.

ANNUAL SEED HEADS

Annuals which produce seed heads need to be sown every year, unless you allow them to self-seed. They should be sown during April and May in the open ground. They are an extremely useful and decorative source of dried flower material.

Amaranthus (love-lies-bleeding)

The amaranthus family are included as seed pods, although love-lies-bleeding is usually thought of as a flower. However, the long red or green ropes or tails of love-lies-bleeding must not be picked until they have set seed, otherwise they will shrink away to a piece of ragged string when dry. Before picking make sure the rope feels firm and plump. Cut just beyond the bend, and leave the plants to grow side shoots for later picking. Hang over a coat-hanger or line to dry.

A. 'Prince's Feather', 'Green Thumb' and 'Pygmy Torch'

The tall amaranthus 'Prince's Feather' and the dwarf 'Green Thumb' and 'Pygmy Torch' must all have the seeds set and feel firm before being picked. 'Green Thumb' and 'Pygmy Torch' have very little stalk, so push a stub wire up the stem before drying.

Candytuft

Candytuft, when well grown, produces strong spirals of seed pods which are good for drying green.

Nicandra (shoo-fly)

Shoo-fly or nicandra is a tall spreading annual, sometimes growing to 3 feet square, with green or green and black lantern-like pods hanging down along the branches. It is much sought after for fresh or dried flower arrangements. Pick it when the pods are fully developed but still green or black. Later they can be picked when brown, or even skeletonized. Remove the leaves, and bunch and hang to dry in a dark place.

Nigella (love-in-a-mist)

Another annual which looks lovely planted between perennials is the pale blue nigella or love-in-a-mist. This plant produces large oval and spiked green and browny purple seed pods which are best picked while still green. Do not strip off the fine feathery leaves.

Opposite: A collection of green seed pods ready to be dried. From centre top: the thin spikes of sweet rocket, a heavy head of lupin pods, the lantern-like green and black shoo-fly pods, the yellowish Jacob's ladder, heads of oriental poppies, more Jacob's ladder, the greyish-green pods of annual poppies and the fancy pods of love-in-a-mist.

Nicandra
(shoo-fly)

Candytuft

Nigella
(love-in-a-mist)

An autumn basket of hosta leaves, annual green shoo-fly lanterns and orange
Chinese lanterns (*Physalis francheti*).

Poppies

The brightly-coloured large and small annual varieties of poppy look lovely planted among perennials in a border. They produce stiff round or oval seed pods that are excellent picked when well mature but still green. Bunch and hang to dry. The leaves can be rubbed off after they are dry.

COLOURFUL SEED PODS

Iris foetidissima (stinking iris)

The bright orange berries of *Iris foetidissima* or stinking iris, found in some chalky woods in October and November, should not be picked until the pods are all splitting open. The bright orange berries remain shiny and waxy for some months. They still look very good when they eventually shrivel but remain in the open pods.

You don't have to search for wild ones, as *Iris foetidissima* is easily grown in your own garden.

Physalis francheti (Chinese lanterns)

Physalis francheti, more usually known as Chinese lanterns, is a wonderful brightener for any arrangement. Pick when all the lanterns have turned orange, and either lay them flat in a box or stand them up to dry.

SEED PODS FROM PERENNIAL PLANTS

Acanthus

Acanthus spikes are the finest of tall seed heads, but sometimes they grow so huge (up to 6 feet tall) that it is difficult to fit them into any arrangement. On these occasions it is necessary to pick them when the seed has set in the bottom half and the top half is still flowering, thus preventing more growth. This way they dry green instead of brown.

Aconitum (monkshood)

Aconitum or monkshood has seed heads similar to those of delphiniums. Aconitum seed heads should not be dried, however, as the seeds and all other parts of the plant are very poisonous.

Allium albopilosum (A. christophii)

Some alliums have breathtaking seed heads, and are worth growing specially for drying. One of the most amazing is the huge balloon-like head of *Allium albopilosum* (*A. christophii*), which is made up of dozens of small lilac-coloured shiny stars on stems. These should be picked just after flowering, while still colourful but showing the seed pod.

A. cernuum and A. siculum

The 12-inch high *Allium cernuum*, with its entrancing head of lilac pink tubular drooping flowers, and the much taller *Allium siculum*, with its unusual clusters of greeny lilac hanging flowers, both produce eyecatching seed heads. As they go to seed these alliums turn their flower stems up to the sun, and eventually dry facing upwards. They are very unusual and attractive in a flower arrangement. Pick them when they have gone to seed.

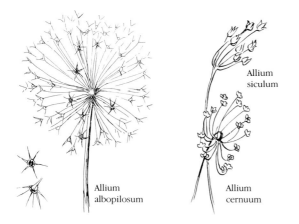

Allium siculum

Allium albopilosum

Allium cernuum

A. sphaerocephalon

The drumstick allium, *Allium sphaerocephalon*, needs to be picked before it loses its plummy red colour and as soon as the top flowers have set seed. Hang in bunches to dry.

Bulbs

Seed heads from bulbs are seldom thought of as drying material, but some can be very attractive. These include bluebells, daffodils, grape hyacinths, and lilies. They are best picked when absolutely ripe.

Grape Hyacinth

Daffodil

Aconite

Canterbury bell and mallow

Canterbury bells and mallows of various kinds have very interesting complicated 'cup and saucer' seed heads. Both should be left in the garden until they have become skeletonized.

Centaurea

As soon as its flower dies, the yellow *Centaurea macrocephala* produces an attractive spherical head made of shiny light brown scales.

Cynara cardunculus (cardoon)

The 6-foot tall silver-leaved cardoon, *Cynara cardunculus*, which is similar to the purple-flowered edible artichoke, develops spectacular seed heads. Pick them as soon as the purple flower has faded to brown. When dry, the dead brown stamens can be removed to reveal the biscuit-coloured centre surrounded by the shining calyx. If you miss picking at this stage and

Cardoon

pick it later, the calyx will fall off leaving a giant powder puff. Both versions are very exciting.

Dictamnus (burning bush)
Dictamnus or burning bush has an intriguing fir-tree-shaped spray of open-triangle seed pods. However, it is not the easiest of plants to grow! It prefers good alkaline soil. Pick when the seed heads burst open.

Doronicum (leopard's bane)
Early in the year, delightful seed heads can be obtained by picking the tall stems of doronicum or leopard's bane as soon as the flowers fade, in May. You will end up with tiny cream powder puffs when dry. These are one of the first flower seed heads to be ready to pick.

Eranthis
Eranthis, the winter aconite, one of the first flowers to brighten the winter with the promise of spring, produces an equally early intriguing little opened seed head in May.

Fritillaria imperialis and F. persica adiyaman
Fritillaria imperialis (the crown imperial fritill-ary) and *F. persica adiyaman* have wonderful sprays of exciting seed pods. Leave them until they are fully mature before picking. Stand them up to dry in not too warm a place, and save the seed for sowing as soon as they split open.

The intriguing little seed pods of *Eranthis hyemalis*, the winter aconite. One of the first seed pods to look out for in May.

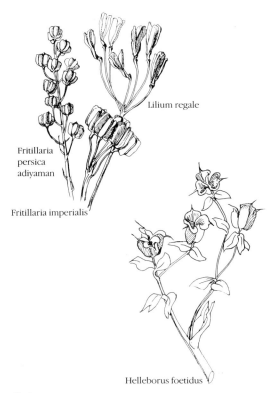

Lilium regale

Fritillaria persica adiyaman

Fritillaria imperialis

Helleborus foetidus

Helleborus
Some hellebores produce fascinating open seed pods, almost like empty honeycombs. It is prob-ably best to cut them short and wire them, as they tend to dry facing in different directions and look untidy.

Hemerocallis (day lily)

The day lilies (hemerocallis) have similar seed heads to those of lilies. Do not pick them until the seed heads split open. Some varieties, however, do not produce any seed heads at all.

Hosta

Some hostas have very decorative seed heads. The best variety is *Hosta sieboldiana*, which splits open to show its shining black seeds. Do not pick until the autumn, when the pods begin to split.

Iris

Yellow water iris or bog iris produces beautiful open silvery curled pods and sometimes keeps its light brown seeds in them after drying. Do not pick the iris seed heads before they begin to split open on the plant. Many other irises have different shaped seed pods useful for drying, but, again, 'splitting time is picking time'!

Lupin

Lupin seed heads have heavy spikes of many pea-like pods which are covered in silky grey hairs and need picking when the seeds are well developed. However, the tree lupin is best left until it has shot away all of its seed, then the pods become attractively twisted like corkscrews.

Paeonia delavayii and P. lutea (tree peonies)

The large starfish-shaped pods of the tree peony, *Paeonia delavayii* and the twin-podded *P. lutea*, split open to show large shining black seeds which unfortunately drop out. However, they reveal an even more exciting mahogany-like interior to the pods, which dry beautifully. The pods must have all begun to split open before they are picked. They will not open if picked before.

Primula, polyanthus and cowslip

Candelabra-type primula seed heads make lovely whirls of round seed pods. *Primula florindae*, polyanthus and cowslips all have pendular flowers which become attractive

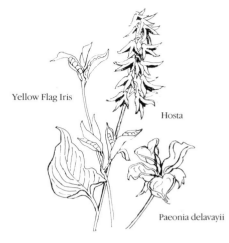

Yellow Flag Iris

Hosta

Paeonia delavayii

upward-facing clusters of seed pods when ready to dry.

Other perennials of interest are asphodeline, delphinium, foxglove, galtonia, hollyhock, red hot poker and verbascum, which all have impressive tall spiky seed heads with differently designed seed pods.

The star-shaped seed pod of *Paeonia delavayii* must not be picked until it has split open.

CLEMATIS

The clematis family is large and varied, and has such a variety of colour and habit that they can fit into all types of gardens. The majority of them have superb seed heads that can be dried most effectively.

Clematis seed heads can be air-dried so that they go fluffy, hair-sprayed so that they stay silky, or varnished to look and feel like an over-lacquered hair-do!

Large-flowered clematis
The large-flowered clematis produce superb single seed heads, and it is these that can be varnished or sprayed with hair lacquer as soon as they are picked. A few of the largest flowers can be dried if caught just before the petals fall off. Dry with care, laid in silica gel.

Clematis macropetala
Clematis macropetala is one of the first clematis to be ready to dry. Wait until the silky green seed heads have a bit of body to them and feel slightly firm, then pick either singly or in sprays. Picking will not harm the plant but will in fact do it good, as next year's flowers will appear on this year's new growth.

C. montana
The *montana* type of clematis have rather sparsely seeded heads, and definitely need to be picked in sprays when the seeds are half developed.

Clematis tangutica and C.t. 'Bill Mackenzie'
In the autumn the yellow bell flowers of *Clematis tangutica* turn to a froth of soft silvery green seed heads. Either use hair-spray and dry, or just allow to dry indoors. The variety 'Bill Mackenzie' has thick lemon-peel-like flowers and produces similar seed heads.

All clematis seed heads must be picked while green and silky. If they have already gone fluffy, they will fall to bits when dry.

SEED HEADS FROM TREES

In a hot dry summer, trees seem to fear for their lives and hurriedly produce millions of nuts or seeds to guarantee the continuation of their kind. This is a wonderful opportunity to gather superb dried-flower material.

Alder, ash and oak
Three trees that have interesting seed pods to dry are alder, with brown oval knobbles, ash, with bunches of green keys, and oak, with lovely acorns and sometimes oak-apples too.

Beech
Beech seed pods, or mast as they are called, should be picked early while they are still tightly closed, and stripped of leaves. When dry, they will open up keeping their nuts intact.

Hornbeam
The hornbeam tree has a very decorative arrangement of seed pods that look like lanterns. Pick small branches and strip off the leaves. They will stay green if dried in the dark, otherwise they will go a sandy colour. These make a most exciting addition to a large arrangement.

Larch
Fir cone sprays from larch trimmings are always lovely, and can look quite ethereal when found covered in lichen in damp woods.

Opened, glycerined beech mast nestles below glycerined old man's beard and dried larch cones.

Lime

If you have access to mature lime trees, their hanging drumstick clusters of seeds make good material for glycerining, after the leaves have been removed. They can also be dried, but tend to fall to bits.

Sweet chestnut

The prickly green seed cases of the sweet chestnut dry very well, but are best glycerined together with their leaves. Both turn a rich brown colour.

BERRIES

Everywhere one looks during the autumn there is a wealth of colourful berries, and one longs to dry them all. Unfortunately there are very few that are really good for this purpose.

Asparagus fern

The red berries of the female edible asparagus fern will last indefinitely if picked when the berries are really ripe. Hang sprays of berries in a warm place.

Clerodendron trichotomum

The most exciting berries of all are those of *Clerodendron trichotomum* – however, it will only grow in acid soil. If it flowers early enough it will produce crowd-stopping clusters of turquoise berries set in stars of crimson calyces. Unfortunately they fade a bit when dried, but they are still well worth doing.

Iris foetidissima

You may find *Iris foetidissima* growing in woods.

After drying it keeps its bright orange berries for some months and still looks good when they finally shrivel. Do not pick until the pods are splitting.

Rose hips

Some of the small cluster-type rose hips dry reasonably well.

Dry all berries in a very warm place, having removed all the leaves first, and store them where mice cannot get at them.

As you walk round the garden or down the road, it is well worth while glancing at each flowerbed or hedgerow you pass, as there are so many interesting seed heads to be found. Excellent seed pods can be found growing wild and also in the vegetable garden. I have written about these in greater detail in the chapters on Wild Flower Seed Heads (p. 67) and The Vegetable Garden (p. 72).

9
WILD FLOWERS

I N THESE DAYS OF intensive cultivation and 'weed'-killing sprays, wild flowers have become few and far between so it would be wrong to pick certain varieties even if you can find them. However, there are a few that thrive on waste ground and beside the road, and no one will object to your picking some of them before the council cuts them down.

WILD FLOWERS GROWING IN DAMP PLACES

Hemp agrimony
One of the most commonly found where the soil is damp is hemp agrimony, with its large fluffy pink heads. It should be picked as soon as the main flower head is in bloom. Stripped of leaves and hung upside down in bunches, they will dry and fade to a beigy pink with green flecks, and the end result is very attractive.

Meadowsweet
Meadowsweet, with its fluffy, cream, scented flowers, is another prolific grower, usually on damp land. This can be dried either in its flowering stage or when the green seeds have formed. In both cases remove the leaves, and stand upright to dry.

Mugwort
Even more widely distributed, and frequently found growing in large grey clumps on the roadside, is mugwort – the wild form of artemisia. This should be picked as soon as the tiny yellow flowers are out. Do not strip off the very attractive silver and black leaves. Hang or stand them up to dry.

Polygonum bistorta and water mint
The deliciously scented water mint and the tall spiked *Polygonum bistorta*, which grows in damp meadows or near rivers, have pink flowers which dry very well. Both should be picked when the flowers are fully out. Bunch and hang them up to dry.

Polygonum polystachyum (Himalayan knotweed)
The 4–5-foot tall *Polygonum polystachyum*, with delicate white flowers on many branched stalks, is also called Himalayan knotweed. Pick the short flowering sprays, bunch and hang. This plant flowers from August until the frosts cut it down.

Purple loosestrife
The perennial purple loosestrife or *Lythrum salicaria* grows in damp meadows or waste places. The tall magenta spikes can be very useful in arrangements. Pick when most of the flowers are out. Stand them upright to dry.

The pink spikes of *Polygonum bistorta*, often found in damp meadows near rivers, make excellent dried flowers.

WILD FLOWERS GROWING ON DRY GROUND

Golden rod

The yellow flowers of golden rod are excellent for drying. The true, highly perfumed wild flower is not often found, but garden escapes are fairly common. Pick when fully out, and stand it up to dry.

Greater knapweed

Greater knapweed has purple cornflower-like flowers and is to be found growing prolifically on downland or beside hilly roads. Pick when fully out.

Great mullein

The tall silvery spikes of great mullein can either be picked when flecked with their yellow flowers or left until they have seeded, when they lose some of their grey colour. These are biennials, so always leave some to seed.

Mullein plants are the food of the elusive mullein moth, and are occasionally covered in brightly spotted caterpillars. In the old days the large grey felt leaves were used as dressings for wounds. These plants like to grow in poor light soil.

Heather

On heathland you will find various types of heather. All need to be picked before the whole spike is in flower, otherwise the flowers will drop when dry.

Marjoram

In drier grassy places in midsummer you may well find the deliciously aromatic wild marjoram, which has sprays of magenta pink flowers. Bunch and hang up to dry. The sprigs of green foliage can also be dried.

Tansy

In waste places or hedgerows you will sometimes find the clustered yellow button flowers of the tansy, a rather unpleasant-smelling plant, which luckily loses most of its aroma when dry. Do not strip off the attractive curled leaves. Pick when the 'buttons' either are yellow or have turned black.

Scented mayweed

On the edge of cornfields or in farmyards you may be lucky enough to find the scented mayweed. This is a deliciously perfumed spray of small yellow-centred white daisies about 12 inches high. It is not so very special to look at when dry, but is well worth tucking into your arrangement for the perfume alone, and is lovely in a pot-pourri.

Thistle

Thistle heads can be wired, if you are brave, and dried easily. Always leave some to seed, as some of them are biennials and can only reproduce by seeding.

SEASIDE PLANTS FOR DRYING

Statice, thrift and sea holly

Near the sea you may find the blue or white limonium (the wild statice or sea lavender) and the delightful wild thrift, with its dwarf pink flowers. Sea holly (*Eryngium maritimum*) makes a lovely dried flower, but I believe this is now becoming rather scarce, so do not pick it – make do with the cultivated kinds.

Here I would like to include a reminder for all collectors of wild flowers. No matter for what purpose you pick them, *never* pick when there is only one flower, in fact never pick many of anything. Some flowers are perennial and would flower year after year even if you did pick the lot, but many are annual or biennial and rely entirely on their seed for their continued existence.

10

WILD FLOWER SEED HEADS

THERE ARE WELL over 1,000 different wild flowers in the British Isles. Many will grow only in specific parts of the country, while others will grow anywhere, provided the soil and conditions are correct. A few will grow anywhere regardless of soil and conditions, and these are usually considered to be weeds.

If a weed has an attractive seed head, let it grow in your garden and harvest it for your dried flower arrangements. Many wild flowers can be grown from seed and sometimes it may be possible to buy plants of the useful seed-head producers and grow your own. Perhaps you may be lucky and find many of the useful varieties growing nearby in the wild, while you may find others when away from home or on holiday.

WILD FLOWER SEED HEADS FOR GLYCERINING

There are three wild flower seed heads that I like to glycerine – the wild *Clematis vitalba* (often known as old man's beard or traveller's joy), hops, and ivy.

Clematis vitalba (old man's beard)
Old man's beard glycerines best if picked when about half developed, with the silky, curly bits short and firm and the seeds tinged red. Hold the spray of 'beard' at the top tip, and pull off the leaves downwards, making sure not to break or bend the stem as this will prevent it drinking the glycerine. Make a fresh cut at the bottom of the stem, and immediately put it into the glycerine mixture for 5–7 days. The seed heads then stay soft and silky instead of going grey and fluffy.

Old man's beard can also be dried to very good effect. If you pick it just as it finishes flowering, strip off the leaves, and hang it up, you will get tiny little white pom-poms. Enchanting! Picked at any other stage it will dry fluffy, as long as it has not already turned fluffy on the

plant – it is then too late! All the fluff would just blow away.

Hops
Disentangling an armful of old man's beard is bad enough – unravelling a huge twisted mass of hops is far, far worse, though very worth while in the long run.

Treat the hops with glycerine in order to prevent the clusters becoming too brittle. Do not leave them for too long after picking, and take care to get the lower end of the stem immersed in the glycerine.

You can also hang hops up in the dark to dry, in which case they will stay green, or allow them to go a lovely apricot beige colour in strong light.

Ivy
Use the stiff erect sprays of ivy with the seed pod just developing. Keep the leaves on, as they also glycerine beautifully.

WILD FLOWER SEED HEADS FROM WOODS

Bluebells

Early in the summer the bluebell woods provide masses of dry spiky seed heads. Do not pick them until they have opened and shed their seeds. The stems are so fragile that they are difficult to arrange, so insert a stub wire up the hollow stem. They are then strong enough to be stuck into a block of Oasis.

Figwort

Even later in the year, stems of green and black 'ball-bearing' seed pods develop on the fig-wort plants. These will dry green and black. Hang up or stand to dry.

Figwort

Foxglove

From August onwards you will find the tall spikes of foxglove seed pods, which make most effective seed heads if picked while still green and stood up to dry. Short side shoots are useful for small arrangements. Hang these up to dry.

Hypericum

From November and on through the winter, in woods, in waste places or on downland, you will find various chestnut-brown seed head sprays of hypericum, the wild St John's wort. These are excellent mixed with blues, yellows or oranges in an arrangement.

Paul compares a first year young teasel plant with the tall ripe teasels it will grow into the following year. This plant is a biennial so leave a few heads to seed.

Stinking iris

Woods are home to various kinds of seed heads. On chalky ground *Irish foetidissima* is very prolific. It has large pods of bright orange waxy seeds which don't shrivel for some months (and even when they do they still look good). Do not pick them until the pods start to split open – generally in late November and December.

Teasel

This is probably the best known seed head to be found in woods and on waste ground. I call it the birds' pub plant. Each set of leaves up the stem is joined to the opposite set, forming a deep bowl which always holds a good tablespoon of water even during a severe drought. The stems of the teasel are cruelly prickly, but the 3–4 inches that rise out of the leaf 'bowl' are quite smooth and free from thorns, so making it safe for a bird to land there or a pheasant to reach up and have a drink. In time the birds shake the plant, and so scatter the ripe seeds.

Pick your teasels as soon as the two rings of lilac-coloured flowers have gone. Remove the prickles with the back of your secateurs, hang or stand them to dry, and they will remain green. They can also be picked just before they flower. Later in the year they can be picked when they have turned brown, but please be sure always to leave some to seed. They are biennial – growing one year and flowering, seeding and dying the next.

SEED HEADS TO BE FOUND ON OPEN LAND AND WASTE GROUND

Cow parsley, eltrot, cow parsnip, and sweet Cicely

Many members of the *Umbelliferae* or cow parsley family make attractive seed heads for drying. Eltrot or cow parsnip has a heavy seed head, green or sometimes tinged with purple. Sweet Cicely has ¾-inch long black seeds which point skywards when ripe and are most attractive. Pick them before they turn black, to avoid them dropping when dry.

Cowslip

The cowslip, *Primula veris*, which unfortunately nowadays is not very plentiful, has a most striking seed head. When they are ripe, the drooping flower stalks become stiff and stand upright. The seed pod then opens and reveals a black hole surrounded by a golden ring. Shake out any remaining seed beside the plant after picking.

Evening primrose

On waste ground or very poor pasture you may be lucky enough to find the evening primrose, *Oenothera biennis*, growing wild. In September it has tall elegant spikes with many inch-long upward-pointing seed pods. Pick when these split open, allowing them to spread their seed first, as they are biennials.

Evening Primrose

Greater knapweed

Producing lovely silver stars, the greater knapweed or *Centaurea scabiosa* is found growing

The shining stars of the greater knapweed, which should be picked before the
rain dulls their brightness.

Centaurea

on chalky grassland, or in great shimmering clumps like silver pennies beside the road. Rain can quickly damage the shine on these seed heads, so pick them as soon as they have opened. Remove any brown leaves before standing them up to dry.

Sorrel
Making a russet glow in old pastures or on downland turf, the spikes of sorrel provide good

dried flower material if picked when well mature.

Teasel
See p. 69.

Wild mustard, penny cress, and garlic mustard
At the edge of cornfields, on arable land, among root crops or near farm buildings, you may find the spiky seed pods of wild mustard or the round flat discs of penny cress. These are all best dried green.

Garlic mustard is a taller member of the same family. This has thin spiky seed pods which make an attractive background for other flowers. Pick while still green. Leaves from this plant are garlic-flavoured, and can be added to salads instead of a garlic clove – very useful for people who find the real thing indigestible.

Wild poppies

Occasionally the seed heads of the scarlet wild poppies can be found. Much of the seed from these will lie dormant for many years, until the soil is redisturbed. This is the reason why one year you will see a sheet of scarlet by the side of a newly made road and the following year there will not be many poppies there. I presume the seed gets washed down cracks into the ground and will not reappear again until the ground is turned over.

SEED HEADS FROM DAMP LAND, BOGGY PLACES AND WATER EDGES

Angelica

Near the banks of rivers you may find the large umbrella heads of wild angelica. The seed heads dry a pale grey green if picked when the seeds are half-developed.

Cotton grass

On boggy moors and sour damp land the wild cotton grasses flourish. These produce lovely unusual white tassels like lumps of cotton wool. They are easy to dry if you stand them up.

Flag iris and water plantain

On the edge of rivers or ponds the yellow flag iris flourishes. Pick the seed pods when they start to split open, and as they dry they will open to show beautiful silvery interiors. In the same type of location you can also find the large and delicate Christmas-tree-shaped sprays of common water plantain seed heads. They can be a decoration on their own.

Giant hogweed

The giant hogweed, *Heracleum mantegazzianum*, is 10 feet high and has a 6-foot spread of seed heads. It is very spectacular but very dangerous – the sap from this plant will unfortunately bring you out in an extremely nasty rash which is difficult to cure. Always wear gloves if you want to handle this plant, and be careful not to let the huge leaves touch your face, or to let the sap to splash on to you when you cut it down.

The giant hogweed has another disadvantage. There are so many seeds to the head that one seeding from a plant can result in a forest of vast 9-foot-high poisonous plants that smother other plants and shrubs. Exciting as it looks, I do not advise drying it.

Meadowsweet

Beside rivers and ponds or beside the road where the ground is damp, you will see in September the tall sprays of gnarled green seeds of filipendula or meadowsweet. These can be picked green, with the cream side shoots still in flower.

There are many other wild flower seed heads, both large and small, growing in their own particular environments. If you wish to pick them, make sure that they have already shed their seed. In that way you can be sure of doing no harm to nature's wonderful garden.

11
THE VEGETABLE GARDEN

UNFORTUNATELY THE person tending the vegetable garden often seems to be far more interested in uprooting any vegetables that are left over, or have not quite reached the required standard for eating, than in leaving them to go to seed for drying. However, I am sure he or she can be persuaded to leave you a few plants when you explain how lovely they will look, and what fun they will have telling their friends what is in your arrangement.

Nogs bunching and stringing parsley for hanging to dry.
Beside her is sweet cicely and in the basket are artichoke
leaves and more parsley. Some of the purple chives have
already been wired and stood in a jar for drying.

In the centre of the picture artichokes dried in flower; on the right the dead stamens have been removed to show a shining calyx, and on the left is an even more mature head with the calyx removed to look like a giant powder puff.

by hanging them singly in a really warm place. Do not remove the leaves, as they dry into lovely twisted shapes.

Alternatively, as soon as the flower has faded to brown, pick your artichoke as a seed head. When it is dry, pick out the brown bits to reveal the biscuit coloured centre surrounded by the bright shining calyx. If you miss picking at this stage and cut it even later, the calyx will fall off and leave you with a huge powder puff – all very exciting.

Asparagus

Asparagus grows into 3-foot feathery ferns. I do not pick the foliage until late summer, otherwise it will shrivel. You will also damage the plants if you pick too early. The female plant is not considered to be so good for eating, but it produces spectacular orange-scarlet berries that dry well and last for years.

Cabbage

Cabbages are seldom allowed to go to seed. After they have produced their attractive yellow flowers these develop into tall sprays of long thin seed pods. If picked while green and dried quickly they lose their smell, and make a very graceful background or foreground contrast for an arrangement. Brussels sprouts have similar seed pods but retain the cabbage smell.

Carrot, fennel, and chives

The leaves and seed heads of carrots and fennel may be dried. Chives are best picked in full flower. The stem of the latter is hollow, and needs a wire up the whole length of it before drying.

Globe artichoke

Most spectacular of all vegetables is the globe artichoke. If you can resist eating them all, and leave a few to produce their magnificent purple thistle-like flowers, you can dry them very easily

Leek

The non-edible tall drumhead alliums make excellent dried flowers, but unfortunately some of them retain a nasty garlicky smell when dry. So we specially grow *Allium porrum*, the edible leek, for its seed heads. These completely lose their oniony smell when dry. Pick when the maximum number of flowers are out, and just as the first seeds set on the top of the spherical white or pink heads, which can grow to 6 or 7 inches in diameter.

Leeks are usually dug up and eaten during the winter, but if, like other bulbs, they are left in the

The leek heads should be picked when the maximum number of flowers are out and the top flowers are just setting seed. The left-hand pink head is ready to pick, while the right-hand one is only just coming into flower.

ground after flowering, they will produce more bulbs and flower again next year.

When we came to live here we were lucky enough to find that Tom, who had looked after the garden for thirty years, would be most upset if he did not come back to do so again. He was a charming, old-fashioned, knowledgeable man who only ventured out of the village under protest when his wife insisted he accompanied her to the shops to buy his clothes and size twelve boots. When he eventually retired, he continued to live across the road and took great pride in growing two lovely patches of leeks for me to dry. After harvesting he would leave them in the ground to multiply and grow again for the following year.

A week before *Gardeners' World* did a programme on our dried flowers, Geoff Hamilton came down to meet us and have a look around. He was very interested to see the crop of leek heads, and hoped Tom would be a helpful addition to the programme. Geoff did his best to get Tom to explain about his perennial leeks, but to no avail. Tom was not going to give away any of our secrets. Finally, in desperation, Geoff asked, 'How do you plant them?' Tom gave him a withering look and said secretively, 'Put 'em in the ground!'

Sadly Tom was not included in the programme and is now, I feel sure, continuing to grow leeks in Heaven.

Parsley

Parsley, when wired into bunches and dried, makes a useful base for an arrangement. It is best picked during late summer and through the winter if not frozen stiff. Earlier leaves tend to be too soft. If left in the ground and allowed to go to

A coloured corn cob, opened out to form a huge 'flower'.

seed but picked before the seed is ripe, it will dry to an attractive honey colour.

Radish

One of the most interesting vegetable seed heads was discovered by my daughter. One spring she planted far too much radish seed and never got round to pulling up the overgrown radishes. She produced, for me to dry, an armful of sprays of beautiful green inflated seed pods. They are quite lovely if you can get them right.

You will have competition for these seed heads in the form of birds. They cannot resist them as soon as the seeds have developed in the pod, which is when you want them too.

Rhubarb

Small branches of the reddish-brown flower spikes of rhubarb can be bunched and hung up to dry. This is best done when the seed has lightly set.

Sweetcorn (maize)

Sweetcorn needs to be left as long as possible on

the plant, until the corn is hard. It will not dry when it is still ripe for eating. There are some fancy kinds specially grown for drying, with yellow, red and even blue corn. There is also a variety called strawberry corn, with small strawberry-shaped orange-brown cobs. They must be sown early in a greenhouse – and pray for a warm summer!

After drying the cob can be opened out, turning each outer husk backwards between thumb and fingers until you reach the 'hairy' bit and reveal the corn inside. It will now look like a huge exciting flower in itself. The tall feathery top of the maize or sweetcorn plant, which is the male flower, makes a lovely light green addition to a fresh flower arrangement if it is picked just after it has flowered and dropped its large yellow stamens. (This happens in midsummer, of course, long before the cob is ready.)

For dried flowers from the vegetable garden do remember not to be greedy; leave one or two of this and that to flower and go to seed.

12
GRASSES

GRASSES AND RUSHES are so numerous and beautiful that they can make fantastic arrangements on their own without other flowers. Many of them can be found growing wild all through the summer, and picking them will not harm the countryside. In fields, hedgerows and damp woods there are many large and small grasses of various shapes which dry beautifully.

A collection of wild grasses. On the left, dried green and glycerined meadow grass. In the centre are dried Yorkshire fog and couch grass. Next is fresh picked, brown topped bent, and the same grass, glycerined a year before. Lying on top of them all is a stem of wild oats, to be dried.

Cotton grass

There are two types of cotton grass which can be found in damp peaty, boggy countryside. Both dry extremely well if picked as soon as the seed heads look like cotton.

Great or lesser reedmace (bullrush)

The great or lesser reedmace is, in fact, the correct name for the bullrush. This is a very unreliable plant for drying, and must be picked very early – even in August – to try to prevent the heads from bursting. To be on the safe side,

spray them with hair lacquer when dry. It's not much fun to find suddenly one day that they have burst into a quite uncatchable beige cloud which is quickly enveloping the whole room.

Meadow grass, Yorkshire fog, tufted hair grass, and brown top bent grass

Some of the more fluffy, open-headed grasses, such as meadow grass, Yorkshire fog, tufted hair grass and brown top bent grass, are better popped into a glycerine mixture for a few days. This prevents them from closing up, as would happen if they were dried in warm air. Instead they turn silky and go golden or biscuit-coloured. If only dried, Yorkshire Fog will remain pink.

Milium effusum

One of the most exciting grasses is the graceful spray-headed *Milium effusum*. This grass grows to 4 feet high and is very common in damp marshy fields or woods. It is best if glycerined for 3–5 days, when it will transform itself into golden silk.

Oats, barley and wheat

Cultivated oats, barley and wheat are excellent for drying. All must be picked while they are flowering or just after, while they are still green. If the seed has become large or ripe it will fall to bits when dry or be eaten by mice.

Reeds, rushes, and sedges

By rivers or sea swamps you can find lovely black or brown plumed heads of reeds, knobbly rushes and drooping sedges. Most can stand up to dry.

Timothy grass, couch, cocksfoot, and quaking grass

Found in meadows, downland and hedgerows, the tall timothy grass, couch, cocksfoot and quaking grass need only be picked green and dried.

Wild oats and barley

Wild oats and wild barley, often found at the

The arching brown heads of a large sedge.

edge of cornfields, dry a beautiful pale green if picked when first out of the sheath, before the seed is formed. Wild oats can be dried standing up to keep the drooping heads in shape.

FANCY GRASSES

Canary grass, hare's tail, and quaking grass

A packet of mixed fancy grass seed is an easy way to obtain useful, unusual, annual types such as canary grass, hare's tail and quaking grass. If possible these should be picked as the little flecks of stamens appear on the head, and in any case they must be picked while still green. They will only take 4–5 days to dry.

Quaking grass is very difficult to pick, as the bobbles twist round each other. You can avoid this happening by keeping it upright as you pick and lift it.

An attractive cultivated grass which would be best stood in a mixture of glycerine and
water for a few days before drying.

Cyperus

Cyperus is an exciting cultivated rush with single
stems supporting a head like an exploding fire-
work. This is a perennial and will develop into a
big clump. It should be hung in bunches to dry.

Pampas grass

Pampas grass (cortaderia) although not wild, is
probably the largest grass to be grown in English
gardens. It can be found in several exciting
varieties and colours. Tall, stiff, fluffy spikes,
flowing pink or gold plumes, all are lovely to
dry. It is possible to glycerine some of the
flowing types of pampas lightly and stop them
from going fluffy. All should be picked as soon as
the plume is out of the sheath, to avoid them
shedding fluff everywhere when dry.

Setaria

Setaria, a grass like millet, should have the seeds
set and be firm to touch before picking.

Squirrel tail

Squirrel tail grass opens up stiff like a bottle
brush when dried, but goes golden and silky if
glycerined.

Most grasses are happy to dry standing upright,
and usually take only 4–5 days in a warm room.
There are many more grasses to be found in the
wild – your best guide is to use what takes your
eye and looks attractive. Just remember to try to
pick them before they set seed, otherwise they
may fall to bits when dried.

13
FOLIAGE AND FERNS

WHEN I FIRST STARTED flower arranging, the fashion was to make a vase or bowl of mixed coloured flowers without foliage. Next single-coloured arrangements were the vogue, and then people got the idea of mixing foliage with the flowers. With dried fresh flowers, foliage is also essential. It can be dried or glycerined, according to the material and the desired final product.

GLYCERINING FOLIAGE

Glycerining considerably changes the colour of the foliage, but it keeps it pliable and it will last indefinitely. Much deciduous, evergreen and herbaceous foliage can be treated in this way.

Choose undamaged material of a shape suitable for your intended flower arrangement, and glycerine it as soon as possible after picking. Mix one part of glycerine to two parts of hot water in a bottle, and shake to mix. Pour into a glass vase or large jar to a depth of about 2 inches. Give the stem a fresh cut straight across immediately before placing in the mixture. Do not bash the stems or damage the bark. Stand it in a light but not sunny place until the leaves change colour, replenishing the mixture if necessary.

The glycerine will clearly be seen working its way up the leaf veins and spreading over the whole leaf until it has completely changed colour. Different types of leaf go different colours, ranging through browns, yellows and blues.

Remove the leaves from the glycerine as soon

Glycerined foliage from three trees. Top left, two different shades of grey eucalyptus, a large spray of light brown oak with a small sprig of beech complete with masts and nuts.

as they have changed colour and stopped drinking. The time this takes can differ from day to day with the same type of tree or shrub. Wet or dry weather, where the plant was growing, and the temperature, all make a difference.

DECIDUOUS LEAVES FOR GLYCERINING

Deciduous leaves and branches can be picked from when they are mature in July until the autumn, when the sap ceases to rise and the leaves turn colour.

Balsam poplar

Balsam poplar is best picked about midsummer, before the leaves get damaged by spots or high winds. This tree has a wonderful scent that pervades the whole garden, first when the buds begin to burst, then when the catkins appear, and finally as the leaves grow. Later in the year the tree has a second growth of scented leaves. After being glycerined the leaves retain this delicious scent. The upper side of the leaf is a very attractive shade of brown and the underside is a lighter liver colour.

Beech

Beech makes a lovely background to an arrangement, so look for a good fan-shaped horizontal branch – easily obtainable off a young tree. Those branches of a mature beech tree that are low enough to pick tend to hang downwards and have upturned ends. This shape of branch will only fit a certain type of arrangement, for example one arranged on a pedestal. Branches from mature trees are often covered in beech mast. Pick these while the mast is still green and closed. They open up as they take up the glycerine, keeping the nuts and revealing silky insides.

After glycerining, beech leaves often turn different shades of brown and sometimes dark green. The state of maturity of the leaves, where they were growing and the weather all seem to make a difference. For instance, leaves growing in deep shade seem to end up a very dark green, while leaves in a sunnier position will turn varying shades of brown. Copper beech will naturally become the darkest brown of all.

Cotoneaster horizontalis

Cotoneaster horizontalis can be picked until the leaves start to take on autumn tints. The tiny leaves turn an attractive shade of light brown, and the elegant fan-shaped branches are beautiful in an arrangement.

Lime

Lime leaves cannot be glycerined, but the winged drumstick-like seeds can, and will stay flexible. Strip off the leaves from the branch before treating.

Oak

Branches of oak glycerine extremely well, but, as with beech, it is necessary to find side branches of young trees. The old branches are not really suitable shapes for arrangements.

Sweet chestnut

In early autumn, when the winds begin to blow, small branches of sweet chestnut are often found lying on the ground. These are ideal for glycerining and are rather fun if they have the prickly seed pods on them. They go a lovely shade of mid-brown. The individual leaves are very large, and can also be used singly in an arrangement.

Whitebeam

When glycerined, whitebeam has lovely light-coloured undersides to its mid-brown leaves. Small branches can be picked until the leaves turn colour and usually glycerine very quickly, in 2–3 days.

EVERGREEN TREES AND SHRUBS FOR GLYCERINING

Apart from eucalyptus, most of the evergreens used for glycerining are shrubs. They are all best picked from autumn to late spring, which is the period when they are not growing their young foliage. As with deciduous greenery, look for and cut suitably shaped branches or sprays that will be useful for an arrangement, and leave them in the glycerine until they change colour.

Bay

Sprigs from a bay tree (which in fact is a bush) usually go a much deeper green when glycer-

Different coloured glycerined foliage shows yellow *Elaeagnus ebbingei*, light brown common laurel with flowers. Dark brown beech with masts and tiny leaved *cotoneaster horizontalis.*

Left: Glycerined foliage from shrubs. On the left is common laurel complete with flowers supporting the dark leaves of *Viburnum davidii.* Above this are the yellow leaves of *Choisya ternata* topped by the spikey mahonia leaf. On the right are the leathery dark brown leaves of Portuguese laurel and in the foreground, yellow leaves of *Elaeagnus ebbingei.*

ined. This also air-dries well, and can then be used in cooking.

Box
The evergreen small-leaved shrub box can be glycerined, but you must look for an old bush with young sprays that have not been clipped. Box can also be dried, when it will retain its original colour.

Camellia
The beautiful shiny green foliage of the camellia is excellent for glycerining. It goes a light brown colour. (This foliage is not allowed into America by the customs officials.)

Choisya (Mexican orange blossom)
Choisya (Mexican orange blossom) is a commonly grown evergreen with apple-green leaves that turn an excellent shade of yellow when glycerined. It is best to use smallish sprays, as the leaves become rather soft. They can be fitted with a false stem to lengthen them if necessary.

Cotoneaster salixifolia
The long sprays of willow-shaped leaves of *Cotoneaster salixifolia* are very useful. Quick to glycerine, they turn a very nice reddish-brown and are ideal for smaller arrangements.

Elaeagnus ebbingei
Elaeagnus ebbingei, the green-leaved silver-backed variety, takes months to glycerine but is well worth waiting for, as it goes deep yellow and silver when ready.

Eucalyptus
The only foliage that does not seem to change colour completely when glycerined is that of the eucalyptus. The species *Gunnii* has small rounded leaves when the tree is young and pointed oval leaves as the tree gets older. They go a slightly darker shade of blue.

Do not be afraid to take the top out of your young eucalyptus tree at 3½ feet high, and again when it reaches 5 feet. This will prevent the tree becoming tall and spindly. Continue to top it frequently, as this will make it sturdy and prevent wind movement breaking the bark on the frozen soil surface in the winter. Use the pruned pieces for glycerining.

Garrya elliptica
The male form of *Garrya elliptica* has the best long silver catkins. In the winter they are at their

best, and they glycerine beautifully together with their foliage.

Ivy
Ivy can be glycerined. The sturdy growth which bears the circular seed heads goes an attractive yellowish-brown.

Laurel
The common laurel and the Portuguese laurel can both be glycerined as the flowers go over. The flowers turn a light brown colour and retain a little of their scent. Both types of laurel can of course be glycerined without the flowers between autumn and spring. The leaves of the Portuguese type resemble and feel like the softest dark brown leather.

Magnolia
Magnolia foliage is not always very easy to glycerine, and it may be necessary to remove the leaves from the twig and immerse them in the mixture in a flat container until they have changed colour. Rinse them and hang up to dry when ready.

Mahonia
Mahonia can either be picked and glycerined immediately or it can be done after it has been in

Common laurel glycerined when in flower.

a vase of water for a time. Glycerine the leaves either separately or in the whole spray.

Stranvaesia
Stranvaesia has neat elongated leaves. It glycerines well, producing a few reddish leaves among the brown.

Viburnum davidii
The small shrub *Viburnum davidii* has a tough leather-like leaf which goes almost black when glycerined.

HERBACEOUS LEAVES AND OTHER MATERIAL FOR GLYCERINING

Bergenia
Bergenia has a large oval leaf. It is essential to wait until the leaf is mature before glycerining.

Epimedium
The heart-shaped leaves of the herbaceous plant epimedium can be glycerined from late summer and throughout the winter. If they stop drinking the glycerine in winter before they are ready finish them by drying.

Moluccella (bells of Ireland)
Moluccella remains green if glycerined for a few days – treated for longer it will go cream. After being glycerined, moluccella will not dry fragile and brittle, as happens with warm air alone, but it will remain pliable. It can then be bleached by leaving in the sun if so desired.

Pussy willow
Pussy willow, in flower, must be glycerined in

early spring before the catkins turn yellow. The catkins will then stay silvery and not fall off.

It is well worth trying out the glycerining process with various items of foliage from your garden, but variegated foliage is better dried. Glycerine is an expensive item, but foliage treated this way will keep for a great many years and can be used again and again.

DRYING FOLIAGE

The colour green, whether in the form of flowers or of foliage, will immediately make any arrangement of dried flowers look fresh, so I like to dry as many things as possible while they are still green.

Branches of variegated foliage such as elaeagnus and pieris should be hung or stood up to dry, according to their shape, to get the leaves hanging naturally on the branch. Stiff sprigs of box and bay are also suitable for drying in this way. Evergreen foliage with white or silver reverse sides to the leaves, such as white poplar, *Elaeagnus ebbingei* and the deciduous silver-backed leaves of wineberry, can all be pressed individually.

Variegated pieris in full flower in April, at which stage it dries well.

HERBACEOUS PLANT LEAVES TO DRY

Artichoke and cardoon

Artichoke and cardoon leaves can be hung in bunches to dry, but will be more effective if laid flat in a very warm place. When nearly dry, stiffen the midrib by passing a long stub wire up the centre of it. The leaves stay a good silver colour.

Crocosmia (montbretia)

The long green leaves of crocosmia or montbretia give a marvellous fresh look to any dried flower arrangement, and need only be hung up in bunches with plenty of room for the warm air to circulate around them. They dry the colour they were when picked.

Cytisus (broom)

Branches of the green stems of broom (cytisus) will dry and remain a dark green.

Epimedium

The branching leaf sprays of the herbaceous plant epimedium are best picked in the middle of the winter while still green or with autumn tints. They can either be part-glycerined and then dried, or dried quickly in good heat, lying flat. They can also be picked when frozen stiff (freeze dried!) and finished in a warm place. They remain green.

Hosta

Hosta leaves dry into wonderful sculptured shapes. They should be picked in early autumn when still green or just beginning to turn yellow, 'fitted' into bunches, and hung in a really warm place until both leaf and stem are dry and stiff. Variegated varieties should be picked in September, while they are still green and the variegations are still clear.

Paeonia (peony)

Mature or coloured peony leaves dry best laid flat – put them between newspaper or under a carpet where they will not be walked on.

Senecio, artemisia and helichrysum

Grey-leaved sub-shrubs such as the senecios, artemisias and helichrysums are all easy to dry by bunching the foliage and hanging up.

Epimedium

Hosta, Sieboldii

Crocosmia

Two yellow dried leaves of *Hosta sieboldiana* beside a white-edged leaf of *Hosta* 'Thomas Hogg'. Two brightly-coloured, ironed creeper leaves and green and gold dried crocosmia leaves complete the picture.

IRONING BRIGHTLY COLOURED LEAVES

Most brightly-coloured autumn leaves, whether picked off a tree or off the ground, can be dried by pressing. A far more effective way of preserving them is by ironing them.

Lay the leaves on blotting paper, set the iron at 'silk' and iron direct on to the leaf. When totally dry and brittle, coat the leaf with a light paper varnish to return its gloss. The leaves can be reassembled back on to their own branch with fine wire or, should they be stemless, given a wire stem. Because the leaves are so brittle it is best to make a small circle with one end of a stub wire and Sellotape it on to the back of the leaf where the stem would have been.

Acer

Brightly coloured acer or maple leaves are excellent for ironing. They usually keep their stems on, making it easy to wire them back on to their own branch.

Parthenocissus tricuspidata (Boston ivy)

The scarlet vine-shaped leaves of the creeper *Parthenocissus tricuspidata*, the Boston ivy,

Brightly coloured ironed leaves. Two types of acer leaf have been wired or glued back onto their own twigs. On the right is an ironed tree paeony leaf. Below leaves of creeper parthenocissus have been (on the left) ironed, wired and varnished (centre) only ironed and (on right) ironed and wired on reverse side.

becomes exceedingly brittle when ironed and always loses its stalk. It must be given a new wire stalk.

Other leaves that iron well are cherry, hydrangea, poplar, rhododendron and vine.

Ironed parthenocissus leaves. On the left, ironed, varnished and wired leaf, (centre) only ironed leaf, (right) a leaf showing the reverse side wired for stem.

DRYING FERNS AND LICHEN

Green or golden ferns are easily dried by pressing or placing upper side down under the carpet. This should be done immediately they are picked, as they quickly curl up when brought indoors. Beware of picking bracken – don't! – for it will be your blood-stained fingers that will need drying! Always cut it with a knife or secateurs.

Ferns should not be picked until they have become mature and firm, many being best picked during the winter. However, some of the larger wild ferns are amusing to dry or press if picked as the brown scale-covered curl of young fern unfolds out of the plant.

Bracken
Most ferns remain green until they die down or get destroyed by snow. However, bracken or brake turns a lovely gold or golden brown colour in the autumn, and must be picked then before it curls up and dies.

The hard shield fern, growing out of a wall among aubrietia and still in good condition for picking in May.

Uncurling young fronds of ferns can be pressed, and make an exciting addition to a dried flower arrangement.

Maidenhair spleenwort and wall rue

The tiny maidenhair spleenwort and wall rue found growing in old stone or brick walls must be picked in late summer. These are lovely for tiny arrangements. Press between two sheets of paper.

Royal fern, Buckler's fern, male fern and lady fern

The royal fern (*Osmunda regalis*) dies down when the frosts come. Buckler's fern, male fern and lady fern are all large and resistant to winter weather, and can be picked in January and February.

Shield ferns and common polypody

Soft shield fern, hard shield fern and common polypody, and the long narrow hard fern growing out of walls or banks or tree stumps can also be picked in winter.

There are many other outdoor and indoor ferns, such as the delicate maidenhair fern, that you can have fun preserving.

The beautiful silver grey lichen found in damp or shady woods or on gnarled old oak trees is easily dried, and is very useful for making a base in a vase or bowl into which you can stick your dried flowers.

SKELETONIZING FOLIAGE AND OTHER MATERIAL

Skeletonizing is the rotting away of the fleshy part of a leaf or seed pod to leave the strong fibrous skeleton outline. This frequently happens naturally, but it can be made to happen by immersing leaves or seed heads in a tub or trough of rainwater for the bacteria to rot away the unnecessary bits.

Late in the year, particularly in a wet season, there are many leaves or seed heads that have been skeletonized naturally where they have fallen or collected in shady damp places. Alternatively make your own skeleton corner.

The large leaves of magnolias and other tough leathery types will skeletonize well. Holly is excellent.

Seed pods of Chinese lanterns, Canterbury bells, poppy and shoo-fly are excellent subjects, and need only be left lying on the ground for slugs and other usually unwanted pests to do their bit. Once they are free of all their rotting bits and have become perfect skeletons, you can lighten their colour by leaving them in the sun or putting them in a mild solution of bleach for a few days.

Brown hydrangea heads will skeletonize if given the same treatment. Divide them up and wire as required.

Holly leaves should be wired with a very fine

Skeletonized Chinese lanterns (top), shoofly (centre), poppy seed heads (bottom).

wire and made into a spray. The shoo-fly skeleton can be opened out, and the Chinese lanterns can be cut up along the ribs with scissors and opened out to make individual 'flowers'.

Radishes can be left in the earth after picking the seed pods for drying, until all the fleshy radish rots away and only the fibrous shape is left. Pull or dig carefully and dry.

Skeleton shapes are very simple to produce, and it will then be up to you to use your own taste and skill in making them into Christmas decorations, pictures or even fairytale flowers.

14
ARRANGING DRIED FRESH FLOWERS

WHAT A JOY IT is arranging dried flowers, and how easy compared with fresh flowers. First, they are so light that even a huge arrangement can be done in quite a light container and not become top-heavy. Second, of course, the stems don't have to be in water – you can lengthen stalks, fix stalks together or just balance a bloom among the others, and having made an arrangement you can always remake it differently or somewhere else a month later if you wish.

CONTAINERS AND OASIS

You probably already have in mind a favourite container in which to arrange your dried flowers. Whatever shape or height it is, I suggest you use the blocks of green Oasis normally used wet for fresh flowers (though of course you use it dry). This is better than the special Oasis made for dried flowers, which is too hard for many of the natural stems of dried fresh flowers. An alternative to Oasis is crumpled wire netting fixed into your bowl or vase. Better still, for a large arrangement, combine the two.

Wedge your block of Oasis firmly in your bowl or vase, allowing the Oasis to be 2–6 inches higher than the rim of the container. By doing this you can arrange your flowers to bend down below the rim. To make an arrangement in a flat dish or on a plate, first visit your local florist and for a few pence buy an Oasis pin holder and some green plasticine to fix the pinholder to the plate. Wedge your block of Oasis firmly on to the pinholder spikes. This will support quite a large arrangement of flowers.

EXTENDING OR REPAIRING FLOWER STALKS

It will often be necessary to extend or repair the stalk of a flower. This can be done in two ways: by using a florist's wire, or, better still, by using a discarded spare stem from another flower. If the flower to be lengthened has a hollow stem, for example a delphinium, just insert a slightly thinner stem (dia A). If the flower has a solid stem, use a hollow one to lengthen it (dia B).

Sometimes when the stems are the same size it is possible to splice them by pushing them very firmly together so that they split into each other (dia C).

The other method of extending or joining a broken flower stem, such as the top of a delphinium or golden rod spike, is to insert a short piece of florist's wire into the top piece of stem,

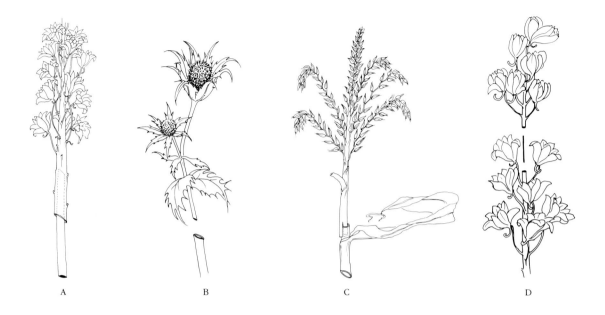

A   B   C   D

leaving enough sticking out to fit back into the bottom stem and make a perfect join (dia D). Hollow-stemmed flowers such as chives should have a long stub wire pushed up their hollow stems and into the head, as soon as they are picked. Seed heads with brittle hollow stems, for example grape hyacinths, can have the wire inserted after drying.

WIRING INDIVIDUAL FLOWERS AND LEAVES

It is often necessary to give a wire extension to a short fragile stem. Take a thin piece of florist's wire, bend down 1 inch of the wire, and place it against the stem of the leaf or flower. Very gently bind the stem and short end of wire together round and down with the long end of the wire (dia E).

Some leaves of the Virginia creeper type are paper thin and very brittle when ironed. They usually have no stems, so it is best to wire them with a medium-weight wire. Bend one end of the wire into a flat loop, shape to the leaf, and sellotape on the back where the stem should be. (dia F). Individual bright autumn leaves can be wired back when dry on to a bare picked branch of the parent tree or better still use a contact glue.

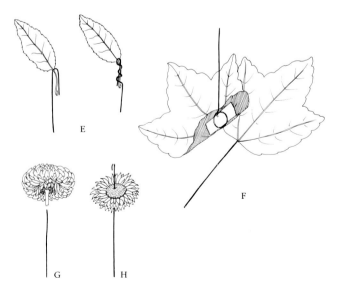

E

F

G   H

Helichrysum and acroclinium flowers are best wired when fresh picked. Although they look much more natural if dried on their own stems, they tend to become floppy on a damp day and spoil the shape of your arrangement.

Wire helichrysums (which should not be fully open when picked) and acrocliniums by cutting off their stems leaving about ½ inch below the head. Pass a medium-weight 8- or 9-inch stub wire up the stem and into the head, being careful not to go too far or it will show as the flower opens when it dries. Stand them in a jar to dry. They will start to open immediately like magic! Roses, African marigolds and other individual flower heads are best wired fresh in this manner (dia G).

Dried heads of helichrysums and acrocliniums can be wired by making a small hook at one end of the wire and passing the long end down through the top of the flower until the hook buries itself in the centre of the flower. This is fiddly, and sometimes the flower falls to bits (dia H). It is better to wire them when fresh if you are doing your own drying.

Dried helichrysums and acrocliniums can be formed into sprays by binding the wires together. Small flowers, for example ageratum, ammobium, gomphrena and rhodanthe, can be wired into small loose bunches to be more effective in large arrangements.

SPRAYING WITH HAIR-SPRAY

Roses, peonies, marigolds and other fleshy flowers which tend to take back some moisture after being dried can be helped by a light spraying of hair-spray. Hair-spray is also a great help for fixing seed heads such as clematis to stop them going fluffy, bulrushes to stop them bursting, and pampas grass if you have picked it too late and it is losing bits and pieces.

DESICCANTS: SILICA GEL AND BORAX

These are drying chemicals, obtainable from a chemist, which make it possible to dry a great many flowers that will not dry by warm air methods. Unfortunately many of these flowers, unless kept airtight or permanently in a very warm place after drying, go limp and discoloured very quickly if the atmosphere is at all damp.

However, some flowers, for example roses picked in open bud stage and astrantia, catananche, dahlias and zinnias picked when full out, are very good dried this way. They shrink far less than when dried by warm air alone.

Cover the bottom of a box (a shoe-box is ideal) with either silica gel or borax, then, using a plastic spoon, carefully work the crystals in between all the petals of the flower to be dried and lay it in the box. When you have got all your flowers in place, completely cover them with more silica gel or borax and leave to dry for 5–6 days. When dry, a light hair-spray can help to fix them. The crystals can be used again and again, occasionally sieving them to remove bits of broken flowers.

15
WINTER DRIED FLOWERS –
WONDERING AND WANDERING

AS YOU SIT by the fire on a winter's evening, occasionally glancing at your rather sad fresh hothouse flowers, dreaming of scented sunny days in your garden among alchemilla and peonies, delphiniums and philadelphus, darting dragonflies and sweetly singing birds, I hope you will take up this book and imagine yourself gathering these fresh flowers for drying, so that you will still have them with you in all their glory for next winter's evenings.

Perhaps you will read a little here and a little there and plan to plant some of the flowers you haven't got already. You could order the seeds for your highlighting annuals, or go and visit a nursery for some special plants with good flowers to dry.

Don't wait for the summer to come to start your dried flower arrangement – start now! All the year round you can find things to preserve. Become a collector – not of foreign stamps but of fresh flowers and foliage. Give a purpose to your daily exercise, whether this is jogging or a gentle stroll, and keep glancing to each side of the path and up into the trees. It's amazing what you will find at any time of the year, and what fun you will have deciding how best to use it.

I do not offer any advice on how to arrange your flowers. Your arrangement should be an expression of your own ideas and feelings with the material that you have collected. What you feel like creating one day may be totally different from what you feel like doing a few days or months later when you have dried more flowers. Well, you can change them – add to the arrangement, swap some of the flowers round, shorten some, lengthen others, re-do the whole thing if you like. The dried fresh flowers won't mind, they will just go on looking fresh and happy.

Take this book with you into your garden. Use the tables at the back of the book and let them guide you in what, when and how to dry or preserve your fresh flowers and foliage, so that you can continue to enjoy your garden all the year round.

Overleaf: Hugh and Paul give the herbaceous border and hedge a manicure while I gather in the early autumn harvest.

TABLE 1

HERBACEOUS PERENNIAL PLANTS AND WILD FLOWERS
What and When to Pick and How to Dry

PLANT NAME AND FLOWER COLOUR	WHEN AND WHAT TO PICK	STRIP LEAVES	STAND ↑ HANG ↓ OR LAY FLAT →	INFORMATION
ACANTHUS (*bear's breeches*) Green-white, tall flower spike	Aug–Nov When flowering, and seeds set below	No	↑ or ↓	Pick while top still in flower.
ACHILLEA (*yarrow*) 'Gold Plate' – yellow 'Moonshine' – pale yellow 'Cerise Queen' – pink 'Sulphurea' – cream 'The Pearl' – white	Aug–Sept With well-matured 'bobble' in middle of each floret Aug Before it goes brown	No	↓ ↓	Will shrivel if picked before developing little 'bobbles' that feel firm. Fades to pink. Spoils in the rain.
ACONITE see ERANTHIS				
ACONITUM (*monksbood*) Blue	July–Aug In flower – seeds poisonous	Yes	↓	These flowers dry very well but are extremely poisonous.
ALCHEMILLA MOLLIS (*lady's mantle*) Light yellow	July–Aug Flower fully out and fluffy	Yes	↑	Younger sprays are smaller but a lighter yellow.
ALISMA PLANTAGO-AQUATICA (*water plantain*) Green/brown wild flower	Sept–Oct When seed is well set	–	↑	A large Christmas-tree-like spray.
ALLIUM ALBOPILOSUM (*A. Christophii*) Mauve	Aug–Sept When seed is set	–	↑	Huge heads, weak stem. Insert thin bamboo up stem.
ALLIUM CERNUUM Drooping greeny mauve flower	Sept Ripe open seed head	–	↑	Dangling flowers, erect seed heads.
ALLIUM PORRUM (*leek*) White/pink spherical heads	Aug–Sept When maximum number of flowers are out and top seeds set	–	↓	Smelly till dry. Part-dry in attic or shed. Finish warm. Very slow to dry. Plants can be left growing and multiplying year after year.

PLANT NAME AND FLOWER COLOUR	WHEN AND WHAT TO PICK	STRIP LEAVES	STAND ↑ HANG ↓ OR LAY FLAT →	INFORMATION
ALLIUM SCHOENOPRASUM (*chives*) Purple	When flower full out	No	↑	Best to insert wire up all stalks when picked.
ALLIUM SICULUM Dangling pink flowers	Sept–Oct When seed head ripe	–	↑	Dangling flowers, erect seed heads.
ALLIUM SPHAEROCEPHALUM (*drumstick allium*) Deep red oval flower heads	Aug When first seed set	–	↑ or ↓	Loses colour if too much seed set.
ALTHAEA (*hollyhock*) Tall spike of flowers Mixed colours	Sept–Oct While seed pod still green or double flowers fully out	Yes	↑ ↓	Tall spike. Round green seed pods. Wire and hang individual flowers.
ANAPHALIS Clusters of white straw flowers	Aug–Sept Early flowering	No	↓	Dwarf and tall varieties – excellent.
ANEMONE PULSATILLA (*wind flower*) Nodding purple flowers	June Pick fluffy seed head before seeds are too large	No	↓	Seed head blows away if seed too ripe. Treat with hair-spray.
ANTHRISCUS (*cow parsley*) Wild flower	June–Aug Press leaves. Green seed heads	Yes	↓ or →	Flowers can be dried for 'filling in'.
AQUILEGIA (*granny's bonnet*) All colours	July–Aug Green mature seed pods	Yes	↓ or ↑	Pods stay green if dried in dim light.
ARMERIA (*sea pink, thrift*) Cushion-like heads of pink flowers	July–Aug Full flower	No	↓	For extra good results, dry in a desiccant.
ARTEMESIA Various varieties Grey foliage, yellow flowers	July–Sept When flowers show yellow	No	↑ or ↓	Leaves attractive when dry
ARTEMISIA DRACUNCULUS (*tarragon*) Green flowers	Aug–Sept Sprays of tiny greeny-black flowers	No	↓	Slightly aromatic filler-in.
ARTEMISIA VULGARIS (*mugwort*)	July–Sept When flowers show yellow	No	↑ or ↓	Leaves attractive when dry
ARUNCUS (*goat's beard*) Large fluffy cream flower spike, 6 ft	May–June Before tips of flower spike fully out	Yes	↑	Similar to a giant astilbe. Will turn brown if whole flower spike full out.

PLANT NAME AND FLOWER COLOUR	WHEN AND WHAT TO PICK	STRIP LEAVES	STAND ↑ HANG ↓ OR LAY FLAT →	INFORMATION
BALLOTA Grey-green whorls of felt flowers	Aug–Sept Pick spike after flowering; should feel firm	Yes/no (see p. 28)	→	Clusters of green felty flowers are bracts. Real flowers are tiny and off-white. Pick before it goes brown. Brittle when dry.
BEAR'S BREECHES see ACANTHUS				
BEE BALM see MONARDA				
BERGAMOT see MONARDA				
BLUEBELL see ENDYMION				
BOG IRIS see IRIS PSEUDACORUS				
CALLUNA (*heather*) Pink, white	July–Nov When two-thirds of the flowers are out	No	↓	Dry away from bright daylight. Rather brittle after drying. Could glycerine for a short time then dry.
CANDELABRA PRIMULA see PRIMULA JAPONICA				
CARDOON see CYNARA CARDUNCULUS				
CARLINA (*Carline thistle*) White	Aug When fully out	No	↓ or →	Trim off dead leaves. Wire heads if dwarf type.
CATANANCHE CAERULEA (*Cupid's dart*) Blue	July–Aug When fully out	No	→	Flowers close when dry. Dry in desiccant for better results.
CATMINT see NEPETA				
CENTAUREA MACROCEPHALA Yellow	July Full flower or seed head	Lower leaves	↓	Goes brown if left too long.
CENTAUREA SCABIOSA (*greater knapweed*) Purple wild flower	Aug–Sept Flower fully out or fully open seed head	No	↑ or ↓	Wonderful star seed heads. They lose their shine with much rain.
CHINESE LANTERN see PHYSALIS				

PLANT NAME AND FLOWER COLOUR	WHEN AND WHAT TO PICK	STRIP LEAVES	STAND ↑ HANG ↓ OR LAY FLAT →	INFORMATION
CHIVES see ALLIUM SCHOENOPRASUM				
CHRISTMAS ROSE see HELLEBORUS				
CIRSIUM Purple	July–Aug Fully out or seed heads	No	↓	Dry on own stalk or wire heads.
COTTON GRASS see ERIOPHORUM				
COW PARSLEY see ANTHRISCUS				
COWSLIP see PRIMULA VERIS				
CROCOSMIA MASONORUM (*montbretia*) Orange	Aug–Nov Mature flower, green or yellow leaves, fully developed seed pod	No	↓	Flowers shrivel but keep colour. Don't bunch too many or green goes yellow. Leaves must be hung in small bunches in a warm darkish place.
CROWN IMPERIAL see FRITILLARIA IMPERIALIS				
CUPID'S DART see CATANANCHE				
CYNARA CARDUNCULUS (*cardoon*) Purple or grey	Leaves any time; flower head green, fully out or seed	No	↓	Dry in very warm place. Dry seed head with calyx on or off like powder puff (see p. 27).
CYNARA SCOLYMUS (*globe artichoke*)	Leaves any time; flower head green, fully out or seed	No	↓	Dry in very warm place. Dry seed head with calyx on or off like powder puff (see p. 73).
DAFFODIL see NARCISSUS				
DAHLIA Decorative or pom-pom flowers	Aug Until frost Full flower	Yes	↓	Medium-sized double flowers. Dry in plenty of warmth.
DAY LILY see HEMEROCALLIS				

PLANT NAME AND FLOWER COLOUR	WHEN AND WHAT TO PICK	STRIP LEAVES	STAND ↑ HANG ↓ OR LAY FLAT →	INFORMATION
DELPHINIUM Blue	June–Nov Full flower before petals drop, or seed head	Yes	↑ and ↓·	Hang spike till it feels papery, then stand to finish drying. Strong colours best. Also use side shoots.
DICTAMNUS (*burning bush*) Pink	Sept–Oct Ripe seed head	No	↑	Very interesting seed head.
DIGITALIS (*foxglove*) Pink/white spikes	Sept–Nov Green or brown seed head	Yes	↑ or ↓	Green seed spikes can be dried or glycerined.
DIPSACUS (*teasel*) Green, mauve	Aug–Dec Immediately after flowers have gone	Yes	↑ or ↓	Can be left to go brown. Rub prickles off stems with secateurs.
DORONICUM (*leopard's bane*) Yellow	June–July As soon as petals shrivel	No	↓	Makes delightful round powder puffs. Or twisted green calyx if left too long.
DOUBLE MEADOW SAXIFRAGE see SAXIFRAGA GRANULATA FLOREPLENA				
ECHINOPS RITRO (*globe thistle*) Blue	Maximum blue colour before flowers open	No	↓	Some varieties very brittle when dry. No good picking after flowering.
EDELWEISS see LEONTOPODIUM ALPINUM				
ENDYMION (*bluebell*)	Sept–Oct As seed pods – split	–	↑	Stems hollow and weak, so insert wire.
EPIMEDIUM Green/yellow	Nov–March Green leaves	–	↓	Either dry or part-glycerine. Can be picked when frozen and dry.
ERANTHIS (*aconite*) Yellow	May–June Open seed pod	No	→	Attractive pods. Pick when seed has gone.
ERICA (*heather*) Pink/white	All year When half of the flower spike is out	No	↓	Rather brittle when dry.
ERIOPHORUM (*cotton grass*) White 'cotton'	June–Aug When it has white fluffy tassels	No	↓	Found in acid boggy places. Very attractive.
ERYNGIUM ALPINA Blue, large flowers	July–Sept As they flower; they lose colour after flowering	No	↓	Wire first flowers.

PLANT NAME AND FLOWER COLOUR	WHEN AND WHAT TO PICK	STRIP LEAVES	STAND ↑ HANG ↓ OR LAY FLAT →	INFORMATION
ERYNGIUM BOURGATII Blue, large flowers	July–Sept Can pick and wire first flowers	No	↓	Pick later flowers in spray.
ERYNGIUM GIGANTEUM (*Miss Willmott's ghost*) Silver	July–Sept Soon after flowering	No	↑ or ↓	Dies after flowering. Leave some to seed.
ERYNGIUM MARITIMUM (*sea holly*) Grey	July–Sept First flowers	No	↑ or ↓	Beautiful grey. Grows near sea. Becoming scarce in wild.
ERYNGIUM TRIPARTITUM Blue, small flower	July–Sept Maximum flower colour	No	↓	Pick small sprays of bluest flowers. Leave others till ready.
EUPATORIUM Dark purple red (HEMP AGRIMONY is the wild form) Pinky green	Aug–Oct When first in flower	Yes	↑ or ↓ ↑ or ↓	Pick whole stems. Flowers mature to pinky green when dry. Side shoots can be picked later when out.
EVENING PRIMROSE see OENOTHERA				
FERNS Green or gold	All year round	No	→	Press under carpet or cushions.
FEVERFEW see MATRICARIA EXIMIA				
FIGWORT see SCROPHULARIA				
FILIPENDULA (*meadowsweet*) Cream or pink	Aug–Nov Full flower or green seed pods	Yes	↓ or ↑	Cultivated and wild varieties. Fluffy flower sprays.
FLAG IRIS see IRIS PSEUDACORUS				
FOXGLOVE see DIGITALIS				
FRITILLARIA IMPERIALIS (*crown imperial*) Orange/yellow	Aug–Sept Ripe seed pod	No	↑	Dangling flowers, upright seed heads. Plant bulb on side.
FRITILLARIA PERSICA ADIYAMAN Purple	Aug–Sept Ripe seed pod	No	↑	Most unusual spray of seed pods.

PLANT NAME AND FLOWER COLOUR	WHEN AND WHAT TO PICK	STRIP LEAVES	STAND ↑ HANG ↓ OR LAY FLAT →	INFORMATION
GALTONIA White	Oct–Nov Ripe seed pod	No	↑	Good seed head for large arrangement.
GIANT HOGWEED see HERACLEUM MANTEGAZZIANUM				
GLADIOLUS All colours	Oct–Nov Ripe seed head	No	↑ or ↓	Lovely in the garden as flowers, very nice as a seed pod.
GLOBE ARTICHOKE see CYNARA SCOLYMUS				
GNAPHALIUM Yellow rock plant	July–Aug	No	↓	Clusters of small yellow everlasting flowers.
GOAT'S BEARD see ARUNCUS				
GOLDEN ROD see SOLIDAGO				
GRANNY'S BONNET see AQUILEGIA				
GRAPE HYACINTH see MUSCARI				
GREATER KNAPWEED see CENTAUREA SCABIOSA				
GYPSOPHILA (*baby's breath*) Several varieties Pink or white	Aug–Sept When maximum flowers out	No	↑ or ↓	Double varieties are excellent for drying.
HEATHER see CALLUNA and ERICA				
HELIOPSIS Double yellow	July–Aug When flowers fully developed	No	↓	Dry quickly in very warm place or wire individual heads.
HELLEBORUS (*Christmas rose*) Flowers Seed pods Leaves	Fully out. Opened pods In winter	No Yes No	→ ↓ →	Dry flowers in desiccants. Wiring small bits could help. Press or lay flat.
HEMEROCALLIS CITRINA (*day lily*)	July–Nov Open seed pod	No	↑	Not all varieties produce seed pods.

PLANT NAME AND FLOWER COLOUR	WHEN AND WHAT TO PICK	STRIP LEAVES	STAND ↑ HANG ↓ OR LAY FLAT →	INFORMATION
HEMP AGRIMONY see EUPATORIUM				
HERACLEUM MANTEGAZZIANUM (*giant hogweed*)	Sept–Nov Very early, before seeds mature, or after seeds have dropped	No	↑	Sap very dangerous, gives bad rash. Plant is biennial, can be invasive.
HESPERIS MATRONALIS (*sweet rocket*) White	July–Sept Mature green seed pod	Yes	↓	Sprays of 4-inch long seed pods. Keep green.
HIMALAYAN COWSLIP see PRIMULA FLORINDAE				
HOLLYHOCK see ALTHAEA				
HONESTY see LUNARIA				
HOSTA SIEBOLDIANA Leaves green Flowers lilac Seed pods brown	Aug–Oct Leaves green or yellow Splitting seed pods	No	↓ ↑	Most hosta leaves dry well. Other varieties have less good seed pods.
HYPERICUM (*St John's wort*) Wild flower Yellow	Sept–Dec Dry seed heads	No	↑	Found in woods or ungrazed wild pasture.
HYSSOP see HYSSOPUS				
HYSSOPUS (*hyssop*) Herb Blue flower	July–Aug In full flower	No	↓	Will grow where lavender won't.
IRIS FOETIDISSIMA (*stinking iris*) Orange	Oct–Dec When all pods have split	No	↓	Pods will not open if picked before they split.
IRIS PSEUDACORUS (*flag or bog iris*) Yellow	Sept–Oct When pods have split open	No	↓	Pods will not open if picked before splitting. Silver interior lost if left too late.
IRIS SIBIRICA Blue	Sept–Oct Ripe open seed heads	No	↑	Some other irises have good seed pods.
JACOB'S LADDER see POLEMONIUM				

PLANT NAME AND FLOWER COLOUR	WHEN AND WHAT TO PICK	STRIP LEAVES	STAND ↑ HANG ↓ OR LAY FLAT →	INFORMATION
LAVATERA (*mallow*) Pink flowers	Sept–Oct Mature green or brown seed head, or skeletonized	Yes	↓	Interesting seed pods. Skeletonize if left in the garden.
LEEK see ALLIUM PORRUM				
LEMON BALM see MELISSA				
LEONTOPODIUM ALPINUM (*edelweiss*)	In full flower	No	→	Small Swiss mountain flower.
LEOPARD'S BANE see DORONICUM				
LIATRIS SPICATA (*blazing star*) Pink/purple	July–Aug Fully out	Yes	↓	Excellent pink spikes.
LILIUM (*lily*) White, pink, yellow	Sept–Dec Open seed pods	No	↑	Many varieties, different shaped seed pods.
LILY see LILIUM				
LIMONIUM (STATICE DUMOSA and S. LATIFOLIA) (*sea lavender*) White or lavender	Aug–Sept Maximum open flower	No	↓ or ↑	All varieties grow best on chalk. Most successful in dry summer.
LUNARIA (*honesty*) Green/purple/silver seed pods	July–Dec Green or purple or dry seed pods	Yes	↓	Very effective picked green or purple. Can then still have pennies stripped out if desired.
LUPIN see LUPINUS				
LUPINUS (*lupin*) All colours	Well set closed pod or open twisted pod	Yes	↓ or ↑	Pick main seed head, leave side shoots to flower and seed. Seed pods covered in grey silky hairs.
LYCHNIS CHALCEDONICA (*Maltese cross*) Scarlet	Open seed head	Yes	↓	Attractive flat clusters. Upright seed pods.
LYCHNIS CORONARIA Magenta	July–Sept When flowers are over	No	↓	Stiff grey stalk and seed pod both good to dry.

PLANT NAME AND FLOWER COLOUR	WHEN AND WHAT TO PICK	STRIP LEAVES	STAND ↑ HANG ↓ OR LAY FLAT →	INFORMATION
LYTHRUM SALICARIA (*purple loosestrife*) Herbaceous or wild flower Purple	July–Sept When fully out	No	↓	Found wild in damp old meadows.
MALTESE CROSS see LYCHNIS CHALCEDONICA				
MARJORAM see ORIGANUM				
MATRICARIA EXIMIA (*feverfew*) Small double flowers, cream/white	Aug–Nov Sprays fully in flower	Only large ones	↓	Dries cream colour. Leave some to seed.
MEADOWSWEET see FILIPENDULA				
MELISSA (*lemon balm*)	Sept–Nov Green seed sprays	Yes, bad leaves	↓	Scented sprays.
MENTHA (*mint*) Apple – mauve Spearmint flower mauve Water (aquatica) Wild – mauve Purple – mauve	Maximum flower spike	No	↓	Other types of mint will dry. All have different fragrances.
MENTHA PULEGIUM (*penny-royal*) Blue	July–Aug Fully flowering	No	↓	Peppermint-scented herb. Dry in the dark to keep green.
MINT see MENTHA				
MONARDA (*bergamot, bee balm*) Red, pink, purple	July–Aug With maximum full flower	No	↓	Flowers shrivel a bit, but good colour. Best dried in a desiccant.
MONKSHOOD see ACONITUM				
MONTBRETIA see CROCOSMIA MASONORUM				
MOSS Green	When looking good; many types	No	→	Choose types with no soil attached. Don't overdry.
MUGWORT see ARTEMISIA VULGARIS				

PLANT NAME AND FLOWER COLOUR	WHEN AND WHAT TO PICK	STRIP LEAVES	STAND ↑ HANG ↓ OR LAY FLAT →	INFORMATION
MULLEIN see VERBASCUM				
MUSCARI (*grape hyacinth*) Blue	July–Aug Open seed pod	No	↑ or →	Very attractive, rather brittle, dry in a box.
MYRRHIS ODORATA (*sweet cicely*) White Green leaves	Sept–Nov Early ripe seed pod Mature leaves	Yes No	↓ →	Seed pods drop if left too long. Attractive green or black seed heads. Keeps aromatic scent.
NARCISSUS (*daffodil*) Yellow	July–Aug Ripe seed head	–	↓	Allow seed to disperse. Interesting shape.
NEPETA (*catmint*) Blue	July–Aug Pick when flower spikes half out	No	↓	Falls to bits when dried if flowers too open.
NERINE Pink	Nov–Dec Dry in vase with a little water	No	↓ or ↑	Small-flowered varieties best.
OENOTHERA (*evening primrose*) Yellow	Mature seed head	Yes	↓	Those with tall spikes usually biennial. Smaller varieties perennial.
ORIGANUM (*marjoram*) Green foliage Purple flowers	Full flower and/or green foliage	No	↓	Scented foliage. Cultivated or wild flower.
PAEONIA (*peony*) Red, pink	June–July First full flower	No	↓	Air dry or dry in desiccant
PAPAVER ORIENTALE (*poppy*) Red, pink	July Ripe or unripe seed pods	No	↓	Different shape and earlier than annual variety.
PENNY-ROYAL see MENTHA PULEGIUM				
PEONY see PAEONIA				
PHYSALIS FRANCHETI (*Chinese lanterns*) Orange	Sept–Dec When all lanterns are orange or skeletonized	Yes	→	Dry where mice can't reach them.
POLEMONIUM (*Jacob's ladder*) Blue, white	Aug–Sept Green seed pod	Yes	↓	Attractive cluster seed heads.

PLANT NAME AND FLOWER COLOUR	WHEN AND WHAT TO PICK	STRIP LEAVES	STAND ↑ HANG ↓ OR LAY FLAT →	INFORMATION
POLYANTHUS see PRIMULA TOMMASINII				
POLYGONUM AFFINE Pink flowers	July–Nov When pink flowers turn red	No	↑ or →	Continuous flowerer, scarlet autumn foliage
POLYGONUM AMPEXICAULE Tall red spikes	Aug–Nov When flowers fully developed	No	↓	Keeps good colour when dry
POLYGONUM BISTORTA (*bistort*) Pink flowers, herb	June–July In full flower	No	↓	Unscented herb, useful pink spike. Can be found wild in damp meadows.
POLYGONUM CAMPANULATUM Frothy pink flowers	July–Frost Fully developed clusters of pink flowers	No	↑ or →	Leaves dry coffee – coloured underneath
POLYGONUM POLYSTRACHYUM (*Himalayan knotweed*) White or pink flowers, wild flower	Aug–Nov or until frost In full flower	No	↓	Tall plant. Pick short sprays of small flowers.
PRIMULA FLORINDAE (*Himalayan cowslip*) Yellow/orange	Oct–Nov Mature seed	No	↑	Dangling flowers. Very attractive upright head of seed pods.
PRIMULA JAPONICA (*candelabra primula*) Red, purple, white	Sept–Nov Mature seed	No	↑	Pick while still green. Sometimes too soft to dry.
PRIMULA TOMMASINII (*polyanthus*)	July–Aug	No	↓ or ↑	Upright heads of open seed pods.
PRIMULA VERIS (*cowslip*) Wild flower, yellow	July–Aug Open seed pods	No	↓ or ↑	Allow the seed to disperse as you pick the seed heads.
RHEUM (*rhubarb*) Red/brown	July–Aug Set seed when good colour	No	↓	Pick small sprays off the main plume.
RUMEX ACETOSA (*sorrel*) Red, pink, green	June–July When flower spike good colour	Yes	↓	Dry very warm to keep colour.
SALVIA SUPERBA Purple	July–Aug Full flower Firm seed pods	No	↓	Various varieties, dries well. Long spires of purple flowers.

PLANT NAME AND FLOWER COLOUR	WHEN AND WHAT TO PICK	STRIP LEAVES	STAND ↑ HANG ↓ OR LAY FLAT →	INFORMATION
SAXIFRAGA GRANULATA FLOREPLENA (*double meadow saxifrage*) White	May–June Full flower	No	↓	Flowers like small white carnations.
SCROPHULARIA (*figwort*) Black or green seed pods	Sept–Dec Well-developed seed pods	Yes	↓	Fascinating spires of green and black spherical seed pods.
SEA HOLLY see ERYNGIUM MARITIMUM				
SEA LAVENDER see LIMONIUM				
SEA PINK see ARMERIA MARITIMA				
SEDUM 'AUTUMN JOY' Red, red-brown	Sept–Nov Full flower or when flower over	Yes	↓	Can dry in arrangement. Takes months to dry completely.
SOLIDAGO (*golden rod*) Yellow	Aug–Sept When fully in flower	No	↑	Must pick before it starts to go brown. Best stood up to dry.
SOLIDAGO CANADENSIS (*wild golden rod*) Yellow	July–Sept	No	↑	Smaller than cultivated form. Lovely scent.
SORREL see RUMEX ACETOSA				
STACHYS LANATA (*lambs' ears*) and STACHYS 'COTTONBALLS'	July–Aug Mature flower spike or leaf	No	↓	The excellent variety 'Cottonballs' has 'bobbles' up spike.
STINKING IRIS see IRIS FOETIDISSIMA				
SWEET CICELY see MYRRIIIS ODORATA				
SWEET ROCKET see HESPERIS MATRONALIS				
TANACETUM (*tansy*) Yellow/black	July–Sept Yellow buttons full out or turned black	No	↓	Attractive but strongly aromatic.

PLANT NAME AND FLOWER COLOUR	WHEN AND WHAT TO PICK	STRIP LEAVES	STAND ↑ HANG ↓ OR LAY FLAT →	INFORMATION
TANSY see TANACETUM				
TEASEL see DIPSACUS				
THALICTRUM Mauve	Aug–Sept Full flower	Yes	↓	Tall, single or double.
THISTLE see CARLINA				
THRIFT see ARMERIA				
TULIP see TULIPA				
TULIPA (*tulip*) All colours	June–July Opening seed head	No	↑	Very attractive.
VERBASCUM (*mullein*) Green/yellow	Well developed in flower, or brown ripe seed head	Yes	↑ or ↓	Tend to become too large. If picked early must be hung up.
WATER PLANTAIN see ALISMA				
ADDENDUM: ERYNGIUM x 'ZABELII JEWEL' Blue flowers	July–Aug First flowers	No	↑ or ↓	Must pick before the blue begins to fade.

TABLE 2

ANNUAL AND BIENNIAL FLOWERS AND SEED HEADS
How to Plant, When to Pick and How to Dry

GH: Sow seeds in greenhouse and plant out X inches apart
OD: Sow seeds outdoors in small pinches at X-inch intervals and thin out to single plants for best results

PLANT NAME, FLOWER COLOUR AND HEIGHT	HOW TO SOW AND PLANT OUT	WHEN TO PICK	STRIP LEAVES	BUNCH AND HANG (↓) OR STAND (↑)	INFORMATION
ACROCLINIUM (*helipterum*) Pink, white, 12″	GH 9″ or OD 9″	Early, in full flower	Yes	↓ or ↑	Natural stem very flimsy. Best wired.
AGERATUM Mauve, 6″	GH 6″	Full flower	No	↓	Plants can be bought.
AGROSTIS NEBULOSA (*cloud grass*) 12″	OD 4″	When stamens appear	No	Stand in glycerine mix for 2 days then ↑	Must pick before seed is ripe.
AMARANTHUS (*Green Thumb*) Green, 12″	GH 8″	When seed is set and feels firm	Yes	↓ or ↑	Wire if no stem.
AMARANTHUS (*love-lies-bleeding*) Red or green, 2–3 ft	GH 10″ OD 10″	When seed is set and feels firm	Yes	↓ on coat hanger or over string	Pick ropes beyond the bend. Leave the rest to grow.
AMARANTHUS (*Pigmy Torch*) Red, 12″	GH 8″	When seed is set and feels firm	Yes	↓ or ↑	Wire if no stem.
AMARANTHUS (*Prince's Feather*) Red, 3 ft	GH 10″ OD 10″	When seed is set and feels firm	Yes	↓ or ↑	Pick ripe spikes first. Leave rest to grow.
AMMOBIUM Small white double straw flowers, 3 ft	GH 12″ or OD 12″	Short sprays, first flower out and large white buds	No	↓	Very prolific all through summer. Very useful.
ASTER Large double daisy, many colours	GH 10″	Pick when full out	No	↓	Wire, or hang in small bunches. Can also be dried in desiccant.

PLANT NAME, FLOWER COLOUR AND HEIGHT	HOW TO SOW AND PLANT OUT	WHEN TO PICK	STRIP LEAVES	BUNCH AND HANG (↓) OR STAND (↑)	INFORMATION
BELLS OF IRELAND see MOLUCCELLA					
BRASSICA (*wild mustard*) 2 ft	OD 6″	Pick well-filled green seed pods	Yes	↓	Other types of this family can be dried.
BRIZA MAXIMA (*quaking grass*) Nodding globules, 12″	OD 8″	Early spring or late summer; pick when stamens appear and grass is still green	No	↓ or ↑	See picking hint in text, p. 77.
CALENDULA (*marigold*) Double yellow or orange flowers	OD 8″	Pick when first full out	Yes	↓	Wire heads if necessary. Good bright colour.
CAMPANULA MEDIUM (*Canterbury bell*) Pink or blue bell flowers, seed pods, 2 ft	GH 12″	Skeletonized seed pods	Yes	↓	Can be skeletonized by leaving in a shady damp garden corner.
CANDYTUFT see IBERIS					
CANTERBURY BELL see CAMPANULA MEDIUM					
CELOSIA (*cockscomb*) Brightly coloured thick upstanding ruffle, 12″	GH 12″	Pick when flower fully developed and firm to touch	Yes	↓ singly in plenty of warmth	A most extraordinary looking flower.
CELOSIA PLUMOSA Plumes of many colours, 15″	GH 12″	Pick when flowers fully developed	Yes	↓ 2–3 stems to a bunch	Dries very bright colours.
CENTAUREA CYANUS (*cornflower*) Double blue/pink flowers on single stems, 2 ft	OD 6″	In first full flower	No	↓	Very double forms best.
CHAMOMILE see MATRICARIA RECUTITA					
CLARKIA Spikes of many bright carnation-like flowers, 18″	OD 8″	Pick when in full flower	Yes	↓	Best grown on chalky soil.
CLARY see SALVIA HORMINUM					

PLANT NAME, FLOWER COLOUR AND HEIGHT	HOW TO SOW AND PLANT OUT	WHEN TO PICK	STRIP LEAVES	BUNCH AND HANG (↓) OR STAND (↑)	INFORMATION
CLOUD GRASS see AGROSTIS					
COCKSCOMB see CELOSIA					
CORNFLOWER see CENTAUREA CYANUS					
DELPHINIUM AMBIGUUM (*larkspur*) White, pink, blue, tall spikes, 3 ft	OD 8″ Hardy annual, can plant previous autumn.	Pick sprays when full out but before petals drop	No	↓	Plant early; damps off in autumn.
DRUMSTICK SCABIOUS see SCABIOSA STELLATA					
FOXTAIL MILLET see SETARIA ITALICA					
GOMPHRENA (*globe amaranth*) Small globe shaped flowers, 12″	GH 8″ or OD 8″	When flowers full out	Yes	↓ in small bunches	Likes to grow on chalky soil.
HARE'S-TAIL GRASS see LAGURUS OVATUS					
HELICHRYSUM (*straw flower*) Mixed colours, 1–2½ ft *H. (Hot Bikini)*, scarlet, 12″	GH 12″ or OD 12″	When flowers large but still closed up	Yes	Bunch tightly and ↓ or wire heads when picked ↑	Dry with plenty of warmth.
HELICHRYSUM SUBULIFOLIUM Single lemon yellow flowers, 12″	OD 6″	Pick when full out	Yes	↓	Small but bright.
HELIPTERUM see ACROCLINIUM					
HORDEUM JUBATUM (*squirrel-tail grass*) Silky, long-haired tassels, 12″	OD 8″	Pick when stamens appear	No	↓ or glycerine for 2 days	Goes fluffy or stays silky.
IBERIS (*candytuft, giant hyacinth-flowered*)	OD 8″	Well-formed green seed heads	No	↓	Pick whole plant.

PLANT NAME, FLOWER COLOUR AND HEIGHT	HOW TO SOW AND PLANT OUT	WHEN TO PICK	STRIP LEAVES	BUNCH AND HANG (↓) OR STAND (↑)	INFORMATION
LAGURUS OVATUS (*hare's-tail grass*) Soft woolly plumes, 15″	OD 6″	Pick when stamens are showing	No	↓ or ↑	Best picked while green.
LARKSPUR see DELPHINIUM AMBIGUUM					
LONAS Flat heads of round yellow flowers, 12″	OD 8″	Pick when full out	No	↓	Good bright yellow.
LOVE-IN-A-MIST see NIGELLA					
MAIZE see ZEA					
MARIGOLD see CALENDULA					
MATRICARIA RECUTITA (*chamomile, scented mayweed*) White daisies, 18″	OD 6″	Pick when in full flower and sunny	No	↓	Not very attractive to look at but delicious scent. Often found wild beside cornfields or in farmyards.
MATTHIOLA (*stocks, double Brompton*) Spikes of highly scented double flowers, 15″	GH 12″	Pick when in full bloom	Yes	Hang individually in very warm place	Keep their scent when dry.
MOLUCCELLA LAEVIS (*bells of Ireland*) Spires of green bells, 2 ft	GH 18″	Pick when bells feel stiff and tiny white flowers are over	Yes	↓ or ↑ or glycerine	Germinate seed at 70°F. Very brittle when dry
NICANDRA PHYSALOIDES (*shoo-fly*) Green or black lantern-like seed pods, 3½ ft	OD 2 ft	Pick while pods still green or black	Yes	↓ sprays of pods	Will skeletonize later.
NIGELLA (*love-in-a-mist*) Light blue flowers with feathery foliage, green and purple seed pods, 12″	OD 6″	Pick flowers when full out; seed pods when green and purple	No	↓	Very useful.
PAPAVER (*poppy*) Large round green seed pods, 1–3 ft	OD 12″	When pods well developed but still green	Yes	↓ in very warm place	Will skeletonize beautifully later in year.

PLANT NAME, FLOWER COLOUR AND HEIGHT	HOW TO SOW AND PLANT OUT	WHEN TO PICK	STRIP LEAVES	BUNCH AND HANG (↓) OR STAND (↑)	INFORMATION
PENNY-CRESS see THIASPI					
PINK POKERS see STATICE SUWOROWI					
RAPHANUS SATIVUS (*radish*) Tall sprays of inflated seed pods, 3 ft	OD	Pick when pods green but full of seed	Yes	↓ well away from mice or birds!	Birds eat the seeds.
RHODANTHE MANGLESII Nodding pink or white straw flowers, 12″	GH 6″ or OD 6″	Pick with first flowers open + large buds	Yes, large leaves	↓ in small bunches	Leave small buds to develop.
SALVIA HORMINUM (*clary*) Spikes of papery pink/blue bracts, 2 ft	OD 6″	When bracts are best colour, firm and papery	Yes, large leaves	↓	Grows best in chalk.
SCABIOSA STELLATA (*drumstick scabious*) Globe-shaped flower and seed head, 12″	OD 6″	After seed set, before seed ripe	No	↓	Falls to bits if ripe.
SCENTED MAYWEED see MATRICARIA RECUTITA					
SETARA ITALICA (*foxtail millet*) Large nodding heads, 18″	OD 6″	Pick when seed is set but not ripe	No	↑ or ↓	Beware of mice eating the heads.
SHOO-FLY see NICANDRA					
SQUAW CORN see ZEA					
SQUIRREL-TAIL GRASS see HORDEUM JUBATUM					
STATICE SINUATA Blue, pink, white and yellow everlasting, 2 ft	GH 12″ or OD 12″	Pick when whole flower head fully out	Only fleshy parts	↓ in warm place	Stems will remain green if dried quickly.
STATICE SUWOROWI (*pink pokers*) 2 ft	GH 10″ or OD 10″	Pick when maximum poker in flower	No	↓	Thrives in wet weather.
STOCKS see MATTHIOLA					

PLANT NAME, FLOWER COLOUR AND HEIGHT	HOW TO SOW AND PLANT OUT	WHEN TO PICK	STRIP LEAVES	BUNCH AND HANG (↓) OR STAND (↑)	INFORMATION
STRAW FLOWER see HELICHRYSUM					
SWEET CORN see ZEA					
THIASPI (*penny-cress*) Wild flower, flat disc seed pods, 12″	OD 6″	Pick when pods still green	Yes	↓	Find in farm waste places.
XERANTHEMUM Amethyst or cream flowers on long stalks, 2 ft	OD 8″	Pick when fully out	No	↓	Unusual colour.
ZEA (*maize, sweet corn*) 3½ ft	GH 12″ or OD 12″ Plant in block	Pick when ripe and hard	Remove ugly leaves	↓	Beware of mice eating them.
Z. Squaw corn, strawberry corn Small oval orange cobs, 2½ ft	GH 10″ Plant early	Pick when hard and ripe	Strip off some leaves	↓ in small bunches	Needs hot summer to ripen.
ZINNIAS Many-petalled flowers, 15″	GH 12″	Pick flowers when fully developed	Yes	Make small bunches and hang or wire individual heads	Can be dried in desiccant.
ADDENDUM: FRENCH MARIGOLD Yellow or orange large variety, 18″	GH 12″	Pick when full out	No	↓	Bunch or wire. Dry very warm. Cool oven excellent.
KOCHIA (*Burning Bush*) Green/red oval plant, 2 ft	GH 18″	Pick when orange/red	No	↓ or ↑	Dry whole plant very warm.

TABLE 3
TREES, SHRUBS AND CLIMBERS
Flowers, Foliage and Seeds for Drying or Glycerining

PLANT NAME AND TYPE	HOW TO DRY OR GLYCERINE	WHEN TO PICK	INFORMATION
ABELIA Deciduous shrub, small leaves	Glycerine small sprays of leaves	Late summer	Useful filler in.
ACACIA DEALBATA (*mimosa*) Tall shrub, feathery leaves, yellow fluffy spherical flowers	Dry sprays of flowers; glycerine green branches of leaves	March–April When two-thirds out in flower; pick leaves when mature	Sprays of mimosa from florists can be dried. The shrub is not very hardy but will grow in the south.
ACER PALMATUM Deciduous tree, small brightly-coloured leaves	Iron leaves on blotting paper	Autumn Bright autumn colours	Varnish with paper varnish to restore shine. Wire on to own twigs.
ACER PSEUDOPLATANUS (*sycamore*) Large tree, winged key-like seed pods	Dry clusters of winged seed pods	Aug–Sept Pick before seeds are fully developed	Clusters of winged pods, often blown off in high winds.
ALDER see ALNUS			
ALNUS (*alder*) Tall deciduous tree, dark brown	Dry seed cones	Autumn and winter	'Cones' stay on trees for long time.
ASH see FRAXINUS			
BALLOTA Small evergreen shrub, grey leaves and flower	Dry sprays with leaves on or off	Aug–Sept After flowers are over	Rain will turn plant brown after flowering.
BALSAM POPLAR see POPULUS BALSAMIFERA			
BAY see LAURUS NOBILIS			
BOX see BUXUS			
BROOM see CYTISUS			
BUDDLEIA 'BLACK KNIGHT' Tall deciduous shrub	Dry purple flower spike, remove leaves	Aug–Sept Full flower	Keeps scent when dry.

PLANT NAME AND TYPE	HOW TO DRY OR GLYCERINE	WHEN TO PICK	INFORMATION
BUDDLEIA CRISPA Low deciduous shrub	Dry sprays of leaves and flowers	Aug–Sept In flower or after	All dry to an attractive grey.
BUDDLEIA 'GOLDEN GLOW' Large deciduous shrub	Dry yellow flower spikes, remove leaves	Aug–Oct In full flower	Useful scented yellow flower spike.
BUXUS (*box*) Very slow-growing shrub	Dry small sprays; slow to glycerine	Any time except when growing foliage	Pick from old unclipped shrubs.
CALLUNA (*heather*) Small evergreen shrub	Hang or stand to dry	Aug–Dec Before flowers are all fully out	Pink/white flowers.
CARPINUS (*hornbeam*) Deciduous large tree with lantern-like seed heads	Dry sprays of seed lanterns; strip off leaves	July–Sept Pick before fully mature	Dry in dark and they remain green.
CARYOPTERIS Small deciduous shrub	Dry bunches of twigs and flowers by hanging	Aug–Sept When blue flowers fully out	Plant likes warm dry alkaline soil.
CASTANEA SATIVA (*sweet chestnut*) Tall tree with large pointed leaves and prickly seed pods	Glycerine short sprays of leaves with or without large prickly seed cases	Aug–Sept Pick when leaves are mature or with small seed cases	Branches often blow off during autumn gales. Goes deep chestnut brown.
CHERRY see PRUNUS			
CHERRY LAUREL see PRUNUS LAUROCERASUS			
CHOISYA TERNATA (*Mexican orange blossom*) Evergreen shrub	Glycerine sprays of foliage	Oct–Apr When not growing young foliage	Goes a lovely yellow colour.
CLEMATIS, LARGE FLOWERED Climber	Dry or glycerine individual seed heads or varnish or spray	Aug–Sept When half developed	Pick only on seed head stems.
CLEMATIS MACROPETALA Climber	Dry or glycerine whole sprays or individual seed heads	May–June When fluffy seed heads half developed	Must pick before it goes fluffy. Goes fluffy when dry, stays silky when glycerined.
CLEMATIS MONTANA Climber	Dry sprays of seed heads	July Pick half ripe seed heads	Remove leaves.
CLEMATIS VITALBA (*old man's beard*) Rampant climber, sprays of cream flowers and curly green seed heads	Dry or glycerine sprays of seed heads, strip off leaves	To dry, pick sprays immediately seed set or later but always before it goes fluffy	To remove leaves, hold tip of spray and pull leaves downwards. Sometimes called traveller's joy.

PLANT NAME AND TYPE	HOW TO DRY OR GLYCERINE	WHEN TO PICK	INFORMATION
CLERODENDRON TRICHOTOMUM Large shrub	Dry clusters of turquoise berries	Oct–Nov Pick when just turned colour	Berries lose some colour when dry.
CORYLOPSIS Small flowering shrub, yellow flowers	Dry sprays of tiny yellow flowers	March–April Pick full out	Can be enjoyed in vase of water first.
COTONEASTER HORIZONTALIS Spreading deciduous shrub	Glycerine flat sprays of leaves	Aug–Oct Until leaves turn colour	Turns mid-brown.
COTONEASTER SALIXIFOLIA Large evergreen wall shrub	Glycerine long thin sprays with berries	Nov–Mar Before new growth	Goes good reddish brown.
CURRY PLANT see HELICHRYSUM SEROTINUM			
CYTISUS (broom) Medium-tall shrub	Dry sprays of green twigs or with flowers on	Twigs any time, or first flowers in spring	Can be dried in natural shape or bent as desired. Light yellow flowered type very good. Interesting filler-in.
CYTISUS BATTANDIERI (pineapple broom) Tall shrub	Dry, scented, yellow flowers	July–Aug When flowers in full bloom	Flowers keep scent when dry.
DEUTZIA Large shrub, double white flowers	Dry double flowers	June–July When full out	Flowers dry cream-coloured.
ELAEAGNUS EBBINGEI Evergreen large shrub, green silver-backed leaves	Glycerine sprays of leaves	Sept–April After or before new growth	Very slow to glycerine, goes good yellow when ready.
ELAEAGNUS VARIEGATA Shrub, yellow-marked evergreen leaves	Dry, hang branches to dry	Any time when shrub looks good and is not growing new shoots	Choose well-shaped sprays when picking.
ERICA (heather) Small or tall evergreen shrub, pink/white flowers	Dry sprays of flowers	Any time when flowering. Pick before all flowers full out	Do not over-dry because the leaves will drop.
EUCALYPTUS Grey-leafed evergreen tree	Glycerine sprays of foliage	Sept–March When not growing new shoots	Leaves go darker grey/blue.
EUONYMUS (spindleberry) Large shrub	Dry small sprays of berries or lightly glycerine	Pick as pods open	Not very good for preserving.

PLANT NAME AND TYPE	HOW TO DRY OR GLYCERINE	WHEN TO PICK	INFORMATION
FAGUS (*beech*) Deciduous tall tree, green or copper leaves	Glycerine flat sprays, press turned sprays	July Till leaves turn colour. Also with green masts	Dark green to copper colouring. Pick horizontal branches.
FRAXINUS (*ash*) Deciduous tall tree	Dry or lightly glycerine seeds	Late summer green; brown bunches of keys	Bunches of 'keys', often blown off tall trees by gales.
GARRYA ELLIPTICA Evergreen shrub with catkins	Glycerine sprays with leaves and long light green catkins	Winter When catkins well developed	Male form of this has best catkins.
HAMAMELIS MOLLIS (*witch hazel*) Large shrub with yellow-tufted flowers	Dry sprays of flowers	Jan–March When flowers full out	Can be dried straight from shrub or left in water until dry.
HEATHER see CALLUNA or ERICA			
HEDERA (*ivy*) Climbing evergreen shrub	Glycerine sprays with or without seed heads	Sept–April When not making new growth	Ivy glycerines to a shiny light brown.
HELICHRYSUM SEROTINUM (*curry plant*) Small grey-leaved shrub, yellow flowers	Dry yellow flowers and grey foliage, hang in bunches	Aug–Oct Yellow flowers or pruned foliage	Has strong smell of curry.
HOP see HUMULUS			
HORNBEAM see CARPINUS			
HUMULUS (*hop*) 20-ft tall twining climber, clusters of seed heads	Dry or glycerine whole sprays	Sept–Oct When mature but not ripe	Green but brittle when dried. Peach coloured when glycerined.
HYDRANGEA 'ALTONA' Large shrub, deep pink-blue mophead flowers	Dry large deep red or purple mopheads and hang in bunches	Sept–Dec When flowers turn red or purple	The best deep pink or blue variety.
HYDRANGEA 'BLUE WAVE' Large shrub, pink-blue lacecap flowers	Dry lacecap flowers; bunch and hang or lay flat	Oct–Dec When flowers become firm and turn pink, blue-grey or green, until frosted	Flowers turn different colours according to amount of sun or shade. Often destroyed by frost before ready to pick.
HYDRANGEA 'EUROPA' Medium/large mophead, flower dusky pink/blue	Dry bun-shaped, green/pink/blue mophead flowers; strip leaves, hang in bunches	Nov–Dec When all florets turn colour or feel firm	Makes unusual colour dried flower. Will grow in dense shade.

PLANT NAME AND TYPE	HOW TO DRY OR GLYCERINE	WHEN TO PICK	INFORMATION
HYDRANGEA 'FRILLYBET' Small shrub, medium bunhead pale pink/duck-egg blue flowers	Dry mature mopheads; strip leaves, bunch and hang in dark warmth	Oct–Nov Mature pale green/blue firm mopheads	Depth of colour of flowers depends on amount of sun or shade.
HYDRANGEA 'GÉNÉRALE VICOMTESSE DE VIBRAYE' Large shrub, light blue/pink mophead flowers	Dry mature mopheads; strip leaves, bunch and hang in warmth	Sept–Dec When flowers turn green/ blue and feel firm	Best blue hydrangea for drying. Continues flowering until frosts.
HYDRANGEA 'GRAYSWOOD' Tall shrub, small pale pink lacecaps turning bright red	Dry mature red lacecaps; strip leaves, lay flat or hang to dry in warmth	Sept–Nov When flowers have turned deep red and feel firm	This plant likes to grow in partial shade.
HYDRANGEA 'HAMBURG' Very large shrub, large deep pink/blue mopheads	Dry mature red/purple mopheads; strip leaves, hang in bunches	Oct–Dec When turned to olive green, deep red or purple	Best hydrangea for colour. Mopheads improve colour as they mature, but heavy rain can suddenly produce brown patches.
HYDRANGEA 'MADAME MOULLIÈRE' Large shrub, white mophead	Dry mature green mopheads; strip leaves, bunch, hang in dark warmth	Oct–Dec When head fully turned light green and feels firm	Best grown in shade. Green mopheads develop red markings in sun.
HYDRANGEA 'PREZIOSA' Small shrub, pink mophead turning bright red/purple	Dry mature mopheads; strip leaves, hang in warmth	Sept–Oct Pick when heads firm and turned to deep red/purple	Best planted out of wind, in sun.
HYDRANGEA 'VEITCHII' Large shrub, best white lacecap flowers	Dry mature lacecap flowers; strip leaves, lay flat or hang in bunches, dry in dark warmth	Oct–Nov When flowers turn lime green in deep shade; will be tinged pink/purple in lighter situation	Best grown in shade.
HYDRANGEA VILLOSA Very large shrub, pink purple lacecap flowers, pink/blue fertile flowers in centre	Dry mature lacecap flowers; strip off leaves, lay flat to dry	When centres of fertile flowers reddish brown and outer florets reddish purple	Best planted in full sun.
IVY see HEDERA			
JERUSALEM SAGE see PHLOMIS FRUTICOSA			
KERRIA FLORA PLENO Large spreading shrub, double deep orange yellow flowers	Dry sprays of flowers; bunch and hang	April–May When in full flower	Kerria keeps excellent colour.

PLANT NAME AND TYPE	HOW TO DRY OR GLYCERINE	WHEN TO PICK	INFORMATION
LACECAP HYDRANGEA see HYDRANGEA 'BLUE WAVE', H. GRAYSWOOD, H. VEITCHII			
LARCH see LARIX			
LARIX (larch) Deciduous fir tree	Dry sprays of small fircones	Winter When needles have fallen, or fallen branches	Lichen-covered old branches are particularly attractive.
LAUREL see PRUNUS LAUROCERASUS			
LAURUS NOBILIS (*bay*) Evergreen shrub	Dry or glycerine leaves	Autumn, winter to early spring	Aromatic, dark green leaves
LAVANDULA (*lavender*) Small grey-leafed aromatic shrub, lavender flowers	Dry sprays of leaves with or without flowers; dry long-stemmed flowers, bunch or lay flat	July or autumn Pick flowers as they come out; dry prunings in autumn	Plants should be pruned every late autumn.
LAVENDER see LAVANDULA			
LAVENDER COTTON see SANTOLINA			
LICHEN Grey 'moss' growing on some branches	Dry on or off branches	Pick any time you find it	Grows best in damp woods or on old oak trees.
LILAC see SYRINGA			
LIME see TILIA			
LUPINUS ARBOREUS (*tree lupin*) Small shrub, yellow/mauve flowers, long seed pods in cluster	Dry seed pods, bunch and hang	Sept–Oct Best when pods become twisted after splitting	This shrub is rather poisonous.
MAHONIA Evergreen shrub, fern-shaped leaves	Glycerine leaves or clusters of leaves	Sept–April When mature	Turns to mid-brown.
MEXICAN ORANGE BLOSSOM see CHOISYA			
MIMOSA see ACACIA DEALBATA			

PLANT NAME AND TYPE	HOW TO DRY OR GLYCERINE	WHEN TO PICK	INFORMATION
MOCK ORANGE see PHILADELPHUS			
OAK see QUERCUS			
OLD MAN'S BEARD see CLEMATIS VITALBA			
OSMAREA BURKWOODII Evergreen shrub, tiny leaves, scented white flowers in early spring	Glycerine small sprays of leaves	Sept–April When not making new growth	A very good garden shrub.
PAEONIA DELAVAYI (*tree peony*) Shrub, dark red single flowers	Dry leaves, lay flat, press or iron; dry seed heads	Oct–Dec Pick leaves when coloured, seed heads when splitting	Seed pods will not open if picked before they split.
PAEONIA LUTEA (*tree peony*) Large deciduous shrub, yellow single flowers	As above	As above	Seed heads have only two pods to each head.
PARTHENOCISSUS QUINQUEFOLIA Climber	Iron leaves very carefully	Pick when turned to autumn colours	This variety has five deep segments to each leaf. Very fragile after ironing.
PARTHENOCISSUS TRICUSPIDATA (*Virginia creeper*) Climber	Iron brightly-coloured leaves	Oct–Nov Pick when turned to red and yellow	This variety has three-pointed vine-shaped leaves. Wire on a new stalk.
PEONY see PAEONIA			
PHILADELPHUS 'VIRGINAL' (*double mock orange*) Shrub	Dry sprays of double flowers; remove all leaves	June–July Pick as flowers fully open	Retains some scent and dries cream-coloured. There is a dwarf variety that also dries well.
PHLOMIS FRUTICOSA (*Jerusalem sage*) Large shrub, grey felty leaves, yellow nettle-like flowers in tiered whorls	Dry flowers with foliage or seed head with foliage; bunch and hang	June–July When part of flower out; seed heads while still green	Some forms of this shrub can cause hay-fever and eye irritation.
PINEAPPLE BROOM see CYTISUS BATIANDIERI			
POPLAR BALSAM see POPULUS BALSAMIFERA			

PLANT NAME AND TYPE	HOW TO DRY OR GLYCERINE	WHEN TO PICK	INFORMATION
POPULUS BALSAMIFERA (*balsam poplar*) Tall deciduous tree	Glycerine sprays of leaves	Midsummer till autumn colours	Beautiful brown scented leaves; underside silver beige.
PORTUGUESE LAUREL see PRUNUS LUSITANICA			
PRUNUS (*cherry*) Small tree, double pink flowers	Dry; hang clusters of double flowers	May Immediately when fully out	Wire back on to own branches.
PRUNUS LAUROCERASUS (*common laurel, cherry laurel*) Evergreen large shrub, panicles of white scented flowers	Glycerine sprays of leaves with or without flowers	Pick when not making young growth, or as flowers go over	Leaves turn light brown. Flowers keep their scent.
PRUNUS LUSITANICA (*Portuguese laurel*) Very large evergreen bush, dark green pointed leaves, panicles of fragrant white flowers	Glycerine branches of leaves with or without flowers	Pick when flowers are going over or any time when not making new growth	Goes a beautiful dark brown, like leather, and flowers keep scent.
PRUNUS SUBHIRTELLA AUTUMNALIS (*winter-flowering cherry*) Deciduous small winter-flowering tree, small pink flowers	Dry sprays of pink flowers	Nov–Feb When flowering	Can be enjoyed in a vase indoors, where it will eventually dry in the warm room.
PUSSY WILLOW see SALIX			
QUERCUS (*oak*) Very tall deciduous tree	Glycerine well-shaped branches	July–Sept When mature but undamaged	Use branches from young tree.
RHUS COTINUS (*smoke tree*) Large shrub, purple leaves and feathery flowers	Dry feathery flowers, glycerine leaves	August When flowers are full out; pick leaves when mature	The less purple-leafed varieties have the best flowers.
ROSA (rose)	Dry blooms; choose bright colours, dry on own stem or wire heads	June–Dec When rose is half to three-quarters open	Choose medium-sized bright-coloured flowers which retain some perfume. Can be dried in silica gel.
ROSA 'DOROTHY PERKINS' Pillar-type climber, sprays of pale pink or red small double roses	Dry spray clusters; remove thorns	July–Aug When last flowers are out	Shake off rain if wet. Dry in very warm place.

PLANT NAME AND TYPE	HOW TO DRY OR GLYCERINE	WHEN TO PICK	INFORMATION
ROSA (*rose*), garnet type Small double flowers	Dry blooms on stems	When rose is three-quarters open	Garnet roses are specially for drying.
ROSA (*rose*), old-fashioned Very double flowers	Dry on own stem or wire; remove leaves	June–July Just before full out	These can also be dried with desiccants.
ROSE see ROSA			
ROSEMARY see ROSMARINUS			
ROSMARINUS (*rosemary*) Small aromatic evergreen shrub, small sharp grey-green leaves and blue flowers	Dry sprays with or without flowers	Pick any time	Can be used in cooking.
RUBUS PHOENICOLASIUS (*wineberry*) Deciduous shrub, long arching branches, pale-backed green hairy leaves	Dry by lightly pressing leaves between paper; hang clusters of red flower heads	July–Oct When leaves are firm Aug, for flower heads	The wineberry fruit is delicious to eat.
SALIX (*pussy willow*) Large deciduous shrub or small tree, silver 'pussy' flowers turning yellow when out	Glycerine sprays of pussies for 5–7 days	March Before the silver pussies turn yellow	When glycerined the pussies do not fall off
SANTOLINA (*lavender cotton*) Small silver-grey evergreen shrub, small yellow button flowers on long stems	Dry flowers or silver foliage, bunch and hang	Pick flowers full out Foliage Sept–April	Very aromatic plant.
SENECIO Medium-sized lax evergreen shrub. Grey leaves, yellow daisy flowers	Dry foliage; flowers best in desiccant	July Pick flowers full out, foliage any time	Not the best shrub to dry.
SMOKE TREE see RHUS COTINUS			
SORBUS ARIA (*whitebeam*) Medium-sized tree, grey/green leaves with grey reverse side	Glycerine sprays of leaves; takes 2–5 days	Aug–Nov Until leaves turn colour	Leaves go beautiful shade of reddy-brown with light coloured reverse side.
SPINDLEBERRY see EUONYMUS			

PLANT NAME AND TYPE	HOW TO DRY OR GLYCERINE	WHEN TO PICK	INFORMATION
SPIRAEA DOUGLASII Tall shrub, fluffy spikes, pink flowers	Dry pink spiked flowers	July–Nov Pick immediately flowers are fully out	Has a main flowering time in Aug, then repeat flowers until frosts.
SWEET CHESTNUT see CASTANEA SATIVA			
SYCAMORE see ACER PSEUDOPLATANUS			
SYRINGA (lilac) Tall shrub, purple double or single scented panicles	Dry short sprays of double flowers, deep colour best; hang to dry in very warm conditions	May–June When first fully out	Keeps some scent.
TAMARISK Medium tall shrub, thin sprays of tiny pink flowers	Dry sprays of pink flowers, bunch and hang to dry	July–Aug Pick when full out	This shrub likes growing near the seaside.
TILIA (lime) Very large tree with drumstick-like seeds	Dry or glycerine drumstick seed heads; strip off leaves, dry flowers	June–July Pick seeds before fully mature; pick flowers full out	The lime is delicately scented.
TRAVELLER'S JOY see CLEMATIS VITALBA			
TREE LUPIN see LUPINUS ARBOREUS			
TREE PEONY see PAEONIA DELAVAYI and PAEONIA LUTEA			
VIBURNUM DAVIDII Low evergreen shrub, large stiff leathery leaves	Glycerine short sprays of leaves until they turn colour	Sept–April When leaves are mature	Leaves go very dark brown with lighter reverse side.
VIRGINIA CREEPER see PARTHENOCISSUS TRICUSPIDATA			
VITIS (vine) Twining creepers with large, five-pointed leaves	Iron brightly-coloured leaves	Oct–Nov Pick when leaves turn bright autumn colours	Set iron at 'silk'; wire leaves when dry
WHITEBEAM see SORBUS ARIA			

PLANT NAME AND TYPE	HOW TO DRY OR GLYCERINE	WHEN TO PICK	INFORMATION
WINEBERRY see RUBUS			

WINTER-FLOWERING CHERRY
  see PRUNUS SUBHIRTELLA
  AUTUMNALIS			

WITCH HAZEL see HAMAMELIS MOLLIS			

INDEX